BAILEIGH HIGGINS

Wake the Dead

Heroes of the Apocalypse - Book 3

First edition

This book was professionally typeset on Reedsy.
Find out more at reedsy.com

Contents

Acknowledgments

Thank you to Alex for the stunning book cover design. You can find him right here on Facebook for more information: 187 Designz

And a shout out to all my family, friends, and fans. Without you, I wouldn't be able to live my dream. I appreciate all of your support and kindness.

Your FREE EBook is waiting!

If you'd like to learn more about my books, upcoming projects, new releases, cover reveals, and promotions, simply join my mailing list. Plus, you'll get an exclusive ebook absolutely FREE just for subscribing!

Yes, please. Sign me up!
https://www.subscribepage.com/i0d7r8

Dedication

This book is dedicated to all the unsung heroes of the world. The men and women who work tirelessly each day to ensure our comfort and safety. Firefighters, paramedics, policemen, doctors, nurses, operators, and more. You are all amazing human beings.

Prologue I - Donna

Donna woke up to find herself shrouded in darkness. The room was quiet, and she could feel the blood rushing through her veins. Her heart beat frantically while she tried to place her surroundings. *Where am I?*

The mattress underneath her felt strange. It seemed unnatural after spending so many days and nights sleeping on the floor of the precinct. Either that or her office chair. Then she remembered. It all came back in a flood of dark and bloody memories: The zombies. Being trapped. Getting rescued. The fire station and the party.

She also recalled feeling ill and going to bed early. Not that the sleep had done her any good because she felt sicker than ever. Her head throbbed, her mouth was dry, and it felt like her bones were on fire. *Oh, my God. It hurts.*

With a groan, Donna slipped out of bed and made her way to the bathroom. She needed to cool off. A cold shower. Anything to relieve the burning sensation that coursed through her veins. Her skin radiated heat, and sweat matted her hair to her forehead.

A dim light in the hallway beckoned, and she stumbled toward it on legs that felt like jelly. The restroom was only a few feet away, and she shoved the door open with a bang.

Pressing one cheek against the cool tiled wall, her hand searched for the light switch.

The fluorescent bulbs flickered to life, and she stepped into the nearest shower stall. With a twist of the knob, a stream of water poured over her head and ran down her body. The icy liquid soaked through her clothes, but she hardly noticed.

Instead, the furnace inside her burned hotter. So hot it felt like her blood had turned into napalm. Sobbing like a child, Donna crumpled to the floor. "Make it stop. Make it stop!"

Her cries echoed throughout the room, and the silence mocked her suffering. She curled into a ball and rocked back and forth. The pain fizzed through her nerve endings. Never had she felt so alone and helpless. *Why does it hurt so much?*

A knock sounded on the bathroom door, and it creaked open. Footsteps rang, followed by the squeak of rubber on smooth tiles. "Hello? Is someone there?"

Donna didn't answer, too wrapped up in the sensations flooding her body. It was hard to focus. Her head felt fuzzy, and her brain wasn't working right. *What's wrong with me?*

"Hello? I heard crying. Is it okay if I come in?" The voice sounded uncertain.

"Who… who's there?" Donna asked, her voice a hoarse whisper.

"It's Sam," the voice answered.

"Sam?" Donna frowned, trying to place the name. Since Frank rescued her from the precinct, she'd met many people, and it was mostly a blur of names and faces.

"Yeah, Sam," he answered with a nervous laugh. "I used to work at Starbucks."

"Starbucks?" Donna replied, shaking her head with confusion.

"I came in with Amelia and Mike. Robert rescued us from their office block," Sam continued. "There was another girl with us called Jane, but she died. Zombies got her."

"W... what?" Donna asked, trying to make sense of his words. They buzzed around her head like angry hornets, and pain razored through her brain. "Ah, it hurts!"

"Are you alright? Can I come in?" Sam asked.

A shadow showed underneath the shower stall's door, and Donna blinked at it through a curtain of wet hair. Another blast of white-hot agony flashed through her nervous system, and every muscle seized.

"I'm coming in, okay?" Sam said, pushing the door open. "I won't look; I promise."

Donna stared at him, her mouth working. She couldn't talk, couldn't respond at all. Her body was a statue.

Sam moved closer, one hand across his eyes. "I'm not looking, I promise."

Suddenly, Donna went slack, and she slumped to the floor. She sucked in a deep breath. "Please, help. Make it stop."

Sam peeked at her through his fingers, saw that she was dressed, and dropped his hands. "What's wrong? Are you hurt? Why are you on the floor?"

Donna reached out one hand, desperate for help. "Please."

Sam fell to the floor next to her and gripped her arm. "Jeez, your skin's like ice."

Donna lay prone, too weak to do more than nod. Her heartbeat slowed, and the fiery heat receded from her body. Goosebumps pebbled her arms, and her lips turned blue. Shivering, she watched as Sam shut off the water and grabbed a couple of towels.

"Here you go. We need to get you warm," Sam muttered

as he wrapped one towel around her shoulders. He used the other to rub her arms and legs to get the circulation going.

"T… thanks," Donna mumbled, huddling closer to his warmth. It felt so comforting, and she pressed her face to his shoulder. The smell of his skin was delicious, and something stirred within her brain. Hunger.

Sam finished rubbing her dry and tossed the damp towel aside. Taking both her hands in his, he said, "Can you get to your feet? We need to get you out of here."

"I can't," Donna whispered, shaking her head. She could feel the strength leeching from her bones. Her heartbeat slowed, and her head lolled back on her shoulders.

"Okay, let me try," Sam said. He attempted to lift her but sagged to the ground after a few beats. "I'm sorry. I'm not strong enough."

"It's okay," Donna said with a weak smile. She meant it, too. It was okay. The pain was gone, and a distant light beckoned to her with its promise of release.

"I'm getting help," Sam said. "I'll be right back."

"No! Stay with me," Donna said, frightened at the idea of being alone. She clung to his hand.

"I really should call someone," Sam said.

"Stay. Just a little while, please," Donna said.

It wouldn't be long now. She could feel it inside her brain. It was like a worm—a parasite burrowing deep into the fabric of her being. Bit by bit, it was taking control until she'd be nothing more than a puppet on a string.

It didn't matter. She was too tired to fight it, and it was only her body. Her soul would join all the other people who'd left this world—her family, friends, and colleagues. The light beckoned, and she gave in with a sigh of relief. Her last breath brushed across her lips. *Time to go.*

Prologue II - Sam

Sam stared at Donna's face, alarmed by her sudden stillness. He shook her once. A gentle nudge. When she didn't respond, he tried again. "Donna?"

Nothing.

"Oh, crap. Is she dead?" Sam cried. He laid her flat on her back and pressed one trembling finger to her throat. "She can't be dead. It's impossible."

When he failed to find a pulse, he pressed an ear to her chest. The silence was both horrifying and deafening. Panic spurted through his veins, and he stared at her slack features with terror. *What do I do? What do I do?*

A flash of memory broke through the fog in his brain, and he remembered a distant CPR lesson from school. Scrambling to remember the details, he checked Donna's airways. She wasn't breathing, and he nodded to himself. "Thirty compressions, two breaths."

He placed both hands on her chest and prepared to begin CPR. Then he paused, realizing he was missing the first step of the lesson: Call 911. Only, there was no call center to phone anymore. No people waiting to dispatch help to those who needed it. Still, he was inside a fire station filled with people more qualified than him to deal with a medical emergency.

Opening his mouth, he yelled, "Help! I need help over here!"

Then he began compressions, just like his instructor had taught him in class. Thirty compressions followed by two breaths. Once he finished a cycle, he paused to call for help once more.

One cycle.

Two cycles.

Three cycles.

Again and again, he tried.

"Damn it. Come on," Sam cried, sweat beading his forehead. His arms were growing tired, and Donna wasn't responding to his efforts. "Is somebody there? I need help!"

Desperate, he bent down for another round of breaths but froze when Donna's eyes snapped open. Their gazes locked, and horror spurted through his veins. Every fiber of his being screamed danger. The instinctive reaction of prey coming face to face with a predator.

The woman he'd tried to save was gone, and a soulless monster had taken her place. Blood-filled eyes locked onto his tender throat, and blueish lips peeled back, baring teeth that suddenly looked very sharp. A deep growl sawed through the air.

"Oh, shit!" Sam jerked backward to avoid the gnashing teeth, but he was a fraction too slow. They closed on his neck and tore into the jugular.

He screamed and tried to pull free, but Donna had him in a death grip. A flash of white-hot agony shot through his brain as his flesh tore apart like wet tissue paper. Blood spurted onto the bathroom floor and splashed across the shower curtain. Each drop heralded his death, and he stared at the crimson pattern with a sense of defeat.

Why did he even bother to fight? People like him didn't survive the apocalypse. In the end, his efforts had been for nothing, and now his struggles were over, just like Jane's.

Chapter 1 - Theresa

Theresa brushed one hand across her brow and blinked. Her eyes refused to focus on the clipboard, and the words swam across the page. A moth flickered past her face, bumping against the yellow bulb of the lamp over and over again. Its suicide attempts went unnoticed by her, absorbed as she was in the dynamics of survival. *There's so much we still need to do. So much we still need to get.*

She ran a finger down the list, checking to see if there was anything she'd missed. The list was pretty complete, but she couldn't afford to overlook anything with so many people under her care.

Medicine, especially antibiotics, antihistamines, painkillers, antiseptics, antifungals, sutures, and hemostatics, were at the top of the list. Surgical equipment, dressings, bandages, creams, and ointments were also essential.

But they also needed food, a solution to the water shortage that was sure to come, and a means to generate electricity. Gardening equipment, building material, weapons, clothes, bedding, and toiletries. It was a never-ending list filled with the things they had to find, make, preserve, or scavenge to survive the apocalypse. Was it even possible?

With a sigh, Theresa pondered the question. Despite her

confident demeanor around the others, she didn't have all the answers. Heck, she didn't have any answers. That didn't mean she didn't need to try, though. It was her responsibility, after all. A burden she'd shouldered willingly.

She reached for another stack of papers but paused when she noticed her empty tea cup. For a moment, she wavered. Should she make more tea and soldier on, or should she go to bed? A glance at the clock and her full bladder convinced her to take the latter route. *Bed, it is.*

Theresa pushed back her chair and stood up. Her back twinged, and she took a moment to rub it with both hands. The soothing motion relieved some of the aches, and she was able to walk after a minute. As much as she longed to take her medicine, she had to wait until she got more stock. Until then, she'd save what she had left for emergencies.

Carrying the empty cup, she exited the office and headed to the kitchen. Halfway there, she heard a loud yell and paused mid-step. Looking around, she frowned. "Hello?"

"Help! Somebody help!" the cry came again, louder and clearer this time.

"Where are you?" Theresa answered as fear set in. While she didn't know what was going on, it couldn't be anything good.

"Is somebody there? I need help!"

The cry for help echoed down the hall, and she pinpointed its location within seconds—the women's bathroom. Breaking into a run, Theresa headed toward the room, her heart banging in her chest. "Hold on. I'm coming!"

"Oh, shit." The words were shrill with terror, and a scream followed seconds later—the cry of a person in pain.

Forcing herself to move faster, Theresa ran down the hall to the women's bathroom. She reached for the door, and her fingers closed around the knob. It felt cold beneath her palm, and she hesitated. What waited inside that room? What horror was unfolding in the heart of their home?

The screams assaulted her ears, and her body responded with a spurt of adrenalin. Driven to action, she shoved open the door and stepped inside. Her eyes swept the open space and fell upon a pair of struggling figures.

She caught a glimpse of a woman's face as her teeth sank into the other person's cheek. The flesh tore apart like paper, and the woman growled with satisfaction while she chewed on the juicy morsel.

Her victim, a young man, batted at her face and hands with his fists but with little effect. He was too weak, a victim of blood loss and shock. A pool of crimson fluid mixed with water formed a halo around his head, and his screams slowly turned to gurgles. With a final gasp, he breathed his last. His eyes glazed over, staring at Theresa with silent horror.

Theresa raised a trembling hand to her chest as recognition flooded her mind. The two on the floor weren't some random strangers. They were Donna and Sam. Innocent bystanders who didn't deserve to end up like that, but the virus didn't care who you were or what you did. It killed without remorse or compromise. A true killer.

Theresa stood frozen on the spot, shaking her head. "Oh, my God. Donna. Sam."

While she hovered outside the bathroom, Andrea appeared next to her, dressed in a rumpled t-shirt and pants. "What's going on?"

Theresa frantically waved her away. "Stay back. It's not safe."

Andrea ignored her, and her eyes fixed on the scene on the bathroom floor. "Is that Sam and Donna?"

"Yes, it's them," Theresa replied, backing away.

Donna's head whipped up at the sounds of their voices, and her gaze shot toward them. She bared her teeth and snarled. A sound so unnatural it sent a shiver down Theresa's spine. She scuttled across the floor like a giant spider, leaving smears of blood in her wake.

"Donna, no!" Theresa cried. She stumbled backward, her legs turned to jelly. Fear left a bitter taste in her mouth, and she forgot about the pain in her back. Stretching out one hand, she tried to push Andrea behind her. "Run! Get help!"

"I'm not leaving you," Andrea said, refusing to budge.

"Don't be stupid. Run," Theresa said.

Donna launched herself through the air, her face contorted. Theresa braced herself for the impact, knowing she was about to die. Unarmed, she was defenseless against the younger woman's attack.

Suddenly, Andrea was there. She slammed both fists into Donna's chest, knocking her back. The woman fell to the floor in a tangle of limbs. Sliding around on the slippery floor, she tried to regain her feet while Andrea flashed Theresa a determined look. "I'll keep her busy while you get help."

"What? No!" Theresa cried, shaking her head.

"Go!" Andrea cried. "There's no time to argue." She pushed Theresa out of the room and closed the door.

As the door swung shut, Theresa caught a final glimpse of Andrea's pale face. Behind her, Donna rose from the floor like a specter of death, her face and body covered with blood.

Frozen to the spot, Theresa stared at the piece of wood that separated her and Andrea. Suddenly, a pair of strong hands gripped her shoulders, and she shrieked. Batting at the hands of her attacker, she whirled around and came face to face with

Robert. Sagging with relief, she grabbed him by the shirt. "Robert. You have to help Andrea!"

"Andrea?" Robert asked with a frown.

"There's no time to explain. She needs your help," Theresa insisted. "Hurry!"

"What's going on? I heard screams," a befuddled Mason asked, appearing next to Robert in the dark hallway.

"It's Donna. She turned and attacked Sam. Now she's killing Andrea," Theresa cried, the words spilling from her lips like poison.

"I'm going in," Robert said, reaching for the door. He pushed it open, but it slammed shut a second later as two bodies rammed into it. He tried again and shoved it open an inch or two. Wild shrieks and yells emanated from the interior, followed by vicious growls.

"Wait," Mason said, grabbing Theresa. "You say Donna's a zombie? And she attacked Sam?"

Theresa nodded. "She killed him. I saw it."

"Then he's infected too, and now… Andrea," Mason said, whirling around. "Robert, wait. Don't open that door."

"What do you mean, don't open it? We have to help Andrea," Robert said, his tone aghast.

"It's too late for her. We have to think of the rest of the station," Mason said.

"Donna? Is that Donna in there?" another voice sounded. It was a shirtless Leo, dragged from his bed by the chaos and the noise.

"Leo, wait!" Mason cried, but it was too late.

Leo threw himself against the door, and his weight combined with Robert's was enough to push it wide open. A bloodied and battered Andrea fell through the opening, a moan escaping

13

her lips.

Donna spotted the frightened knot of humanity gathered in the hallway and threw herself at them. With hooked fingers and gnashing teeth, she attacked Leo. He staggered back under the assault, hard-pressed to keep her away from his naked flesh.

Robert and Mason jumped in to help, and the two wrestled Donna into a semblance of submission. They twisted her arms behind her back and held her in place while Leo grabbed her legs. Together, they dragged her away from the rest of the people in the hallway.

"Andrea," Theresa said, rushing to help. Bite marks marred Andrea's arms and shoulders, each tooth indentation deep enough to touch bone. A flap of flesh hung from one wrist, torn loose by Donna's vicious attack, and a steady stream of blood pulsed from her torn neck.

"Don't worry. I'm here. You're not alone," Theresa said, trying to stem the flow of blood from her neck. It was a useless exercise. The artery was torn beyond repair.

Andrea's eyes fluttered open, and she looked at Theresa. "S… Sebastian. Promise me you'll look after him. He's all I have left."

"I'll look after him," Theresa said, knowing that false platitudes were useless to Andrea now. "I promise."

"What happened?" someone said, and Theresa looked up. The hallway was rapidly filling with people, all scared and confused. She spotted Ruby and waved her over.

"Can we do anything for her?" Ruby asked. "I can get the med kit."

"It's too late," Theresa said, removing her hands from the wound in Andrea's neck. Already the crimson river was slowing as Andrea bled out.

"There must be something…." Ruby said, but her voice petered out as she recognized the truth.

"I'm sorry, Andrea," Theresa whispered, a single tear sliding down her cheek. "You saved my life."

Andrea managed a faint smile, one corner of her mouth twisting up. "I did, didn't I?"

"Yes. You're a hero." Theresa squeezed Andrea's hand. "It'll be okay."

"I… I…" Andrea said before she went still. Silence fell over the room, broken at last by the question they all longed to ask.

"How did this happen?" Ruby said.

"It was Donna."

"But we examined her for infection," Ruby protested.

"I know, but we must've missed something. I must've missed something," Theresa said, guilt welling up inside her chest.

Already the woman she'd known as Andrea was gone, her features losing that essence that made her human. Her mind and soul fled into the night until all that remained was an empty vessel—one teeming with a viral infection.

"We need to quarantine the body," Theresa said.

"I'll get a stretcher," Ruby said.

"Get two. We need to take care of Sam as well," Theresa said, praying they had time to secure the corpses. She wasn't sure how long it would take for the bodies to reanimate. *It takes at least a few minutes, right? We have time, I'm sure.* "Hurry, please."

"Will do," Ruby said. She rushed off, followed by Elijah, Benjamin, and Mike to help her carry the stretchers and, eventually, the bodies.

"We'll need weapons," Frank said, his expression dour. "Just in case."

"Good idea," Theresa said. "The keys to the gun locker are

inside my office. Desk, top drawer."

"Got it," Frank said, hurrying down the passage.

"Thanks, guys. The rest of you should go back to the dorms and close the doors. Stay there until we let you know it's safe," Theresa said.

"You should lock them up inside the bathroom. We can't risk waiting for them to wake up," Amelia said, pointing at Andrea and Sam's bodies.

"I can do that," George said, volunteering.

"Thanks, George," Theresa acknowledged. "The rest of you can go. Shut the doors and wait until we let you know it's safe to come out."

"We can help," Rick protested.

"No," Theresa said with a grim expression. "If this goes any further, we'll need your help. All of your help. We don't know if anyone else has been infected."

"You heard the lady. Let's give them some space," Amelia said, waving everyone back. "Let's go."

The crowd reluctantly followed her orders. All except George, who prepared to drag Andrea's corpse into the bathroom. "Let's get this over with, okay?"

"Okay," Theresa said, wiping her bloody hands on her shirt. She got to her feet and looked around with a frown.

"Something wrong?" George asked.

"Where's Clare?"

"Clare? I don't know. I haven't seen her. Do you want me to look for her?" George asked.

"Yes, but let's secure these bodies first," Theresa said, thinking fast. Who knew what Donna had done before she killed Sam? Who knew who else she might have hurt?

"Agreed," George said, gripping Andrea in a fireman's hold

before dragging her body toward the bathroom.

He made it seem easy, and Theresa watched with relief as he moved through the doorway. Soon, the nightmare would be over. Frank would return with weapons, and they'd take care of Sam, Andrea, and Donna. In the morning, they'd bury their people and mourn their losses. More importantly, they'd learn from their mistakes and be stronger for them in the future. *Mistakes.*

Guilt poured through her veins. The fault lay with her: Missing Donna's infection. Locking all the available weapons away without easy access. Not having a set protocol for such a situation or an effective way to deal with the infected. Even worse, they had no backup plan. No escape route should the worst come to pass. *This is my fault. I thought we were safe here, but I was wrong, and now we have to pay for my mistakes in blood.*

Chapter 2 - Sam

Inside the bathroom, Sam lay prone on the cold tiles. Already, the virus had taken control of his brain, moving faster than usual. The viral load inside his bloodstream quickly overwhelmed the pitiful defenses his slender frame could muster, and his fingers twitched with undead life.

The old Sam was gone along with all of his memories. Nothing remained of the boy he'd been: Idealistic, naive, and a touch lazy. Ambitionless, his father called him. A dreamer was his mother's opinion. They were both wrong, seeing a version of him that existed only in their minds.

The actual Sam wanted nothing more than to succeed in life. He dreamed about fancy suits, shiny cars, private jets, and penthouses, but he lacked the ruthlessness needed to climb the corporate ladder. Though he possessed both the brains and the ambition, he was too kindhearted. The same could not be said of the new him.

Zombie Sam's eyes fluttered open, and he rolled onto his stomach. Without a sound, he climbed to his feet. Agile for a zombie, his slender frame was packed with the vitality of youth. Unhampered by emotion, he felt no pain, no hesitation, no empathy, or love. Only hunger.

A movement drew his attention, and he turned to see a man

back in the room. He was bent over, dragging something heavy. A corpse. Not that Sam cared. Dead meat offered no sustenance to his kind. All he cared about was the living flesh mere yards from his position, and he honed in on his prey. On silent feet, he charged.

Chapter 3 - Mason

Mason held onto Donna's arms with all of his strength. The woman possessed the strength of a demon and threatened to break loose from his grasp with each kick. Judging by their strained expressions, Leo and Robert felt the same.

"God, she's strong," Robert said with a grunt.

"Agreed. What do we do with her?" Mason asked, catching a blow on the chin that caused his jaw to slam shut, clipping his tongue. Blood flowed from the cut, and he swore. "Damn it. Hold still, will you?"

Donna responded with an earsplitting shriek that caused all of them to wince. Thrashing about, she tossed her head and tried to bite anything within reach. Bloody saliva frothed on her lips, and the veins in her neck bulged with the effort.

"Let's just get her down the stairs and into the bay area first," Robert said, his face a deep purple hue.

"Hurry. It's like holding onto an eel dipped in a vat of oil," Leo said, dodging a flying foot.

Together, they wrestled Donna across the length of the building, down the stairs, and into the garage. While Mason and Leo restrained her, Robert searched for a length of rope. He found one and tied her to one of the concrete posts holding the bay roof.

"Phew, that should do it," Robert said, surveying his handiwork.

Donna snapped at him, her teeth closing together with audible clicks. She fought the ropes, wriggling like a worm. Undead, she didn't know when she was beaten.

"What now?" Mason said with a shake of his head. "Do we kill her?"

"She's secure for the moment," Robert said. "We have bigger fish to fry."

"Yes, we should get back," Leo said. "That woman, Andrea, was hurt. If she dies, she'll turn. And what about Sam? Donna killed him, right?"

"We need to be able to defend ourselves," Mason said.

"The weapons are locked up," Robert said, pointing to the weapon's locker. "Theresa's got the keys."

"Not our fire axes," Mason pointed out.

"You're right. Let's grab a few," Robert agreed, walking toward the nearest equipment rack. A shrill scream froze him in place, and he looked at Mason. "What was that?"

"Nothing good," Mason responded, grabbing a weapon. There was no time to gear up, and he sprinted up the stairs two at a time. *Clare. Where's Clare?*

Halfway up, they met Ruby, Elijah, Benjamin, and Mike. They were running toward the screams, stretchers forgotten.

"What's happening?" Mason yelled, grabbing Ruby's arm.

"I don't know," Ruby replied, shaking her head.

"Well, we'd better find out what's going on fast," Robert said.

"Stay behind us, Ruby. We're armed, and you're not," Mason added, brandishing his ax.

"Alright, go ahead," Ruby said, hanging back.

Mason charged down the hallway with Leo and Robert hot

on his heels. They reached the bathroom within seconds and stumbled to a halt. George was pinned to the floor by a rabid Sam while Theresa hovered in the background, helpless.

She spotted Mason and cried, "You have to help George. Hurry!"

"I'm coming," Mason said, forging ahead.

He charged toward the wrestling duo, trying to get in a blow, but Sam spotted him coming. He snarled, blood dripping from his lips as he launched himself into the air. His slender body torpedoed across the hall, heading straight for the hapless Mason.

"Oh, shit," Mason cried, bracing for the coming blow, but Sam hit him with the force of a freight train.

Flying backward, Mason landed on the carpet with a brutal thud. His breath left his lungs in a rush, and he gasped for oxygen. Hands scuttled across his body like crabs, and he lashed out with his feet. That did little to deter the hungry fingers looking for a handhold, and fear pulsed through his veins. He expected teeth to sink into his flesh at any moment, and he'd never felt more scared in his life.

"Mason, hold on," he heard in the background, and relief filled his being. Then Sam was there, snapping at his throat with bared teeth. Relief gave way to panic, and he knew he had to do something fast. His eyes fixed on Sam's thick hair, and he grabbed two fistfuls. "A little help here, please!"

Suddenly, Sam stiffened. His eyes bulged, and a thin stream of blood trickled down his face. An ax stuck up from his skull, and he slid to the side as his muscles went limp. Dead, at last, Zombie Sam slumped to the floor.

"Are you okay?" Robert asked, popping up overhead.

"I'm fine. I think," Mason said, stifling a groan. "I feel like I got hit by a bus."

"It sure looked like it," Robert said. "You went down like a sack of potatoes."

"Thanks," Mason said, allowing Robert to help him up. He looked at Sam's corpse and shook his head. "It's too bad. Poor guy."

"Yes, it's awful, but we've got bigger problems," Theresa interrupted.

"What's wrong?" Mason asked.

"George got bitten."

Chapter 4 - Clare

Clare pulled her jacket close around her body and stamped her feet. The thick fibers barely kept the cold at bay, and each breath puffed from her lips in a cloud of white mist. She tucked her hands underneath her armpits and leaned against the low wall that edged the fire station's roof.

Unable to sleep, she'd been driven out of bed in search of peace. Her head buzzed with the aftereffects of the alcohol she'd drunk, and it caused old memories to surface—bad memories. While the party had been fun, it wasn't something she'd done in years, not *since the overdose.*

Below her stretched the city, shrouded in darkness. A couple of lights shone from a few buildings, and she wondered if they'd been switched on before it all went to hell or if they signaled survivors. If they did, those people were acting pretty dumb, in her opinion. Leaving a light on would only serve as a beacon to the living and the dead.

The fire station was hidden from view, the windows covered by thick shutters and blinds. A couple of dim lights shone inside, enough to navigate should the occupants need the toilet.

The same went for the office block next door with the survivors from the school. They were under strict orders from Theresa not to reveal their existence. Idly, she wondered how long they'd stick to those orders. Not long, probably. From experience, she knew people were rebellious, none more so than herself.

She'd made a lot of mistakes in her life. Some she regretted, some she didn't, but there was one that lingered in her mind. It tainted every thought and action she had from that moment onward. It became a dreadful secret buried deep within her being. Not even Mason knew about it; he never would if she had her way. It would destroy him.

As she gazed at the ruins of Burlington, she couldn't help but wonder if it was part of her punishment. Not the apocalypse itself. That would be pure hubris. No twist of fate or distant deity would be so cruel as to end the world just to punish one person. But surviving the apocalypse? That might just be punishment enough for what she'd done. *If it is, I sure deserve it.*

Clare shuddered. It didn't help to dwell on such things, and she pushed the morbid thought aside. Sitting down on the ledge, she tried to clear her mind. It wasn't easy. With everything going on, there was a lot to consider. Not least of them was how they'd survive the coming days, weeks, and months.

There was so much to do. Even though they'd managed to clear the block and set up barricades, they still needed to secure it for good. Zombies could and would get through the barriers. Especially if they traveled in groups, and she shuddered to imagine what a horde would do to their defenses.

Snipers. They needed snipers on the rooftops, sturdier barricades, twenty-four-hour patrols, and armed guards. But to have that, they required more experienced fighters. People who could handle guns and kill zombies. Plus, they needed more weapons and ammunition.

The latter they could get from the police station. A thorough sweep of the precinct would deliver what they needed. It was risky, but it could be done, as proven by Donna's rescue. All she had to do was convince the rest of the group of the necessity. *I'll bring it up first thing in the morning.*

With that thought in mind, Clare decided to give sleep another shot. It was getting late, and the morning would bring more challenges. A distant scream brought her to a halt as she walked toward the exit.

Frowning, she cocked her head and listened. The screams were faint but distinct. Something was happening inside the station. It could be someone having nightmares. Since the apocalypse, it was pretty standard. Paisley suffered from terrible nightmares, but she wasn't there anymore. She was next door with the kids and the teachers from the school.

Speeding up, she raced across the roof and opened the door to the stairwell. Sound blasted her ears without the thick metal sheet to muffle the effect, and she flinched. Someone was in pain. Terrible, awful pain.

Sprinting down the stairs, she burst into the kitchen and looked around. Several people thundered past in the hallway. Too many to count. Then she spotted Frank and called out. "Hey! What's happening?"

He paused and shot her a calculating look. "You can handle a gun. Follow me."

"But —"

"I'll explain on the way. Hurry," he said, his tone brooking no argument.

At a loss for words, Clare obeyed and followed him to Theresa's office. Once there, he rummaged through the desk drawers until he found a bunch of keys. He dangled them in the air with a resolute look. "Listen up. I'll only say this once."

"Okay," Clare replied, her heart banging in her throat. In the background, she could still hear screams and cries of fright. Something was very wrong. "Where's Mason? Is he alright?"

"The infection got into the station, and several people are down," Frank said, holding up a hand to forestall her questions. "I don't know who or how many, but Mason is safe for now."

Clare nodded as relief surged through her veins. Her brother was safe. That was all that mattered at that moment.

"These are the keys to the weapon's locker. You and I are going to fetch some guns, and we are putting this infection down. Got it?"

"Yes, I understand."

"I don't care who it is or what they mean to you. If they come at you, you put a bullet in their brains," Frank added. "Even if it's your brother."

"I… okay," Clare said, swallowing hard on the knot in her throat. She wasn't at all sure if she could do it, however.

"Come on," Frank said.

He ran toward the stairwell, and they arrived in time to see a knot of people rush past. She spotted Mason among them, carrying an ax, but he was gone before she could make a sound. Hovering at the top of the stairs, she stared at his receding figure. *Mason. Be careful, please.*

"There's no time to waste, Clare. Follow me," Frank said, pulling her attention away from her brother.

"What?"

"The guns, remember?" Frank added.

"Okay. Let's go," Clare said, and they ran down the steps.

At the bottom, they turned toward the weapons' locker

but stopped short when they spotted Donna. She was tied to a pillar and acting crazed, shrieking and screaming like a banshee. Blood covered her face and chest, and her eyes rolled in their sockets.

Realization dawned, and Clare said, "It's Donna. She was the one who got infected."

"Yes, she was," Frank said, his expression bleak.

"And you didn't notice?" Clare asked, anger rising in her breast. "How is that even possible?"

"I don't know. We examined her. So did Theresa and Ruby."

"Clearly, you didn't look hard enough," Clare said, striding past him. "Who did she kill?"

"Sam and Andrea," Frank said.

"Two people? She got to two people?" Clare cried, unable to believe her ears. "We need to set up a few ground rules when this is over. A system for dealing with this kind of shit."

"Agreed," Frank said, removing the key to the locker from his pocket. "But right now, we have work to do."

"You've got that right," Clare said, her anger simmering below the surface. She followed Frank into the locker and chose a loaded shotgun from the rack. Next, she picked up a couple of pistols and tucked them into her belt. "That should do it."

"Are you ready?" Frank asked.

"Let's go," Clare replied with a curt nod.

They exited the locker and headed toward the stairs, cutting across the floor. Donna spotted them and broke into fresh paroxysms. As she struggled against her bonds, one of the knots came undone. The ropes sprang free, and she launched herself at Clare with a snarl.

Caught by surprise, Clare had no time to react. Donna

slammed into her like a ton of bricks, and they went down hard. Hitting the ground with a thud, Clare grunted as pain shot through her ribs and spine. She muffled a cry and grabbed Donna by the collar of her shirt. "Frank, help me!"

"I can't get a shot in," Frank said, his feet dancing around them on the floor. "She's moving too much."

Teeth snapped at her face with ferocious intensity. Clare strained to get away from Donna's hungry maw, but the woman possessed enormous strength. Bit by bit, she drew closer. Bloody saliva dripped from her lips, and Clare shuddered as the cold slime touched her skin. "Do something, Frank!"

"Hold on," Frank said, his feet disappearing from view.

Panic spurted through Clare's veins, and she searched for him without success. "Frank? Where are you?"

Silence.

Donna growled, straining against Clare's grip on her shirt. The flimsy material tore a little, and she inched closer.

"Frank, you asshole!" Clare screamed with horror. She could feel the material unraveling between her fingers, knowing she had mere seconds left to live. "No, no, no!"

With an audible rip, the shirt's collar tore free, and Donna took her chance. She lunged forward with her lips peeled back, aiming for the throat.

Clare threw herself to the side, and the snapping teeth missed by a hair's breadth. "Frank!" Her voice was shrill and unnatural in her ears—the product of extreme fear and panic.

"Coming," Frank yelled.

Suddenly, she heard the sound of running feet followed by a hollow thunk. A flash of silver was all she saw before Donna flew to the side. The woman rolled across the floor before stopping several feet away. Tangled and twisted, she lay on the concrete floor without moving.

Heaving for air, Clare scrambled to her feet. Wide-eyed, she stared at the hammer in Frank's hand before looking at Donna. "Is she dead?"

"She's dead," Frank said with a note of finality.

"Thank God," Clare said, heaving for breath. She wiped Donna's blood and spit away using her sleeve and shuddered. "That was close. Too damn close."

"I'm sorry," Frank said, his voice terse.

Clare looked at him, noting the tight lines around his eyes and mouth. "I know she was your friend, but you didn't have a choice."

"Colleague, not a friend," he deflected.

"That doesn't make it any easier," Clare said.

"No, it doesn't."

"I'm sorry," Clare said, feeling inadequate. Nothing she said could heal his pain, after all. Grief had to run its course. It was just the way of things.

After a few seconds, Frank turned away from the sight of Donna's corpse. He walked toward the stairs, still holding the bloody hammer. "Come on. Our friends need us."

"I'm coming," Clare said, heading after him.

It amazed her how quickly the night had progressed from light-hearted fun to all-out horror. First, they'd had a party, celebrating everything they'd achieved, and now they were mourning the loss of several friends and colleagues. It was messed up, and she knew they'd pay for that night for a long time to come.

Chapter 5 - Bobbi

Bobbi allowed Amelia to hustle her back to the dorm room, but only so that she could fetch her gun from its hiding spot. The same one she'd stolen from the locker room. Somehow, it had been missed, and she'd grabbed the opportunity to steal it away. While the people from the firehouse had been good to her, she didn't believe in relying on others. You either shifted for yourself, or you became a parasite. A tick feeding off the hard work of others.

Moving fast, she ran to her bed and fished out the gun from underneath the mattress. After checking the load, she tucked it behind her belt and pulled on a light jacket along with her boots. With her hair drawn back in a knot, she was prepared to face whatever lay beyond the dorm room door.

"Wait. Theresa told us to stay here," Amelia protested when she saw Bobbi heading to the exit.

"You can do what you want, but I'm not staying here," Bobbi said with a level stare. "I'm not a lamb content to sit here and wait for slaughter."

"I know that. I didn't mean —" Amelia said with a hurt look.

"Out of my way, lady," Bobbi added, ducking outside. She had neither the time nor the inclination to soothe someone's ruffled feathers.

As she stepped into the hallway, screams echoed through the space. They were edged with fear and pain but also anger. Rushing toward the bathroom, she found Theresa standing against the wall with Andrea lying at her feet. Struggling inside the entrance to the bathroom were George and the freshly reanimated Sam.

"Damn it. I knew this would happen," Bobbi muttered as she pulled the gun from her belt. Although she faced exposure for the theft, she had no choice. As practical as she was, she couldn't just stand there and watch someone die. Even if it was George.

Taking a stand, she aimed at Sam's head. It proved impossible to pin him down, however, and she hesitated. If she missed, she risked shooting George. "Damn it. Hold still, would you?"

Suddenly, a chorus of running feet filled the hallway, and a group of people burst onto the scene. First among them was Mason, followed by Leo and Robert. They were armed with fire axes, and hope flared within her chest.

Theresa spotted them, too, and cried, "You have to help George. Hurry!"

"I'm coming," Mason said, charging toward Sam and George. Both were down on the ground, but Sam pounced the moment he spotted Mason.

"Oh, shit!" Mason yelled, but it was too late. They tumbled to the ground with Sam trying to take a chunk out of Mason.

"Hold on, Mason," Robert roared, jumping into the fray. He aimed a short, chopping blow at the wriggling Sam and got in a lucky strike. The razor-sharp blade sunk into the skull and cut through the brain.

Sam stiffened, and his eyes rolled back into his head. A bloody snarl remained frozen on his face as he slumped to the side. The virus inside his brain flashed out as it lost control, unable to survive without viable brain tissue to control. Instantly, it was over.

Only, it wasn't.

While Mason climbed to his feet, George moaned with pain, one hand clutched to a gaping hole in his forearm. Blood pulsed from the wound, and Theresa cried out with horror. She rushed forward and tried to stem the flow of blood with a handkerchief she pulled from her pocket.

Bobbi stared at the delicate floral cloth with a sense of bemusement. It seemed so out of place, not just in the station but in that day and age. *Who still carries handkerchiefs? I bet it's scented too.*

While Bobbi pondered the antiquated habit of carrying handkerchiefs in one's pocket, Robert fussed over Mason.

"Are you okay?" Robert asked.

"I'm fine. I think," Mason said. "I feel like I got hit by a bus."

"It sure looked like it," Robert said. "You went down like a sack of potatoes."

"Thanks," Mason said, allowing Robert to help him up. He looked at Sam's corpse and shook his head. "It's too bad. Poor guy."

"Yes, it's awful, but we've got bigger problems," Theresa interrupted, shooting them a pointed glare.

"What's wrong?" Mason asked.

"George got bitten."

"Oh, shit. What do we do?" Mason cried.

"I don't know. We have to stop the bleeding and clean the wound," Theresa said. "I need a first-aid —"

"There's no time," Bobbi interrupted, and all eyes turned to her.

33

"What?" Theresa asked. Her gaze flashed from Bobbi's face to the gun in her hand, and her eyes narrowed. "Where did you get that?"

"Never mind," Bobbi said. "You have to cut it off before it's too late."

"Cut it off?" Theresa repeated, aghast.

"Just like she did with me," Rick said, appearing at Bobbi's side. He held up his hand, the stumps where his fingers used to be still bandaged.

"But this is his arm we're talking about. Not two fingers!" Theresa said.

"Do you want him to die?" Bobbi asked pointedly.

"No," Theresa said, shaking her head. "Of course not."

"Then you've got no choice," Bobbi said.

"George?" Theresa asked. "It's up to you. It's your choice."

George looked from her to the gash on his arm and swallowed hard. His skin was pale, and a sheen of sweat covered his forehead. "Do it. Just do it."

"Are you sure?" Theresa asked.

"Yes," George said, closing his eyes.

"You'd better hurry before the virus spreads," Bobbi added.

"Okay," Theresa said, a determined look taking hold of her features. "Mason and Leo, carry George to the kitchen table. Robert, grab the med-kit. Susan, light the stove and boil water. Amelia, I need clean towels. Lots of them."

"I'll fetch the whiskey," Rick volunteered. "George will need it."

"Good thinking," Theresa said, wiping her bloody hands on her shirt. "I also need a disinfected saw and a file. Hurry!"

As everyone rushed to obey her orders, Theresa pointed at the gun in Bobbi's hand. "Take care of Andrea. She'll turn soon, and you can't let that happen."

"Okay," Bobbi said, swallowing hard.

She waited until she was alone in the hall before moving closer to Andrea's body. The woman looked like a broken doll, and Bobbi thought of her cat, Sebastian. *Poor creature. He's all alone now.*

The memory of her dogs flashed to the forefront of her mind, and she shuddered. The awful sight would stay with her forever, branded into her soul. She couldn't allow that to happen to Sebastian. "I'm sorry, Andrea. This is the end of the road for you, but I promise to take care of Sebastian."

Andrea stirred, and her eyelids fluttered. A faint smile twisted her lips, almost as if she had heard and understood Bobbi. Her head rolled to the side, and she groaned, the sound inhuman. Andrea was no more, and the time had come.

With a sigh, Bobbi squeezed the trigger. The shot was shockingly loud in the confined space, and she staggered back with a gasp. Her ears sang, and her head spun, a painful combination. Huddled against the wall, she pressed her palms to her ears and waited for the worst to pass.

It took a couple of minutes, and during that time, the entire station was in an uproar. People ran past, their arms loaded with the things Theresa had asked for in preparation for George's amputation.

It was a horrible thought, cutting off the right arm of a fit young man, but it had to be done. Rather than have him end up like Donna, Sam, and Andrea. Still, Bobbi knew she didn't want to witness the operation. Chopping off Rick's fingers had been a spur-of-the-moment decision. Amputating George's arm was a different matter.

When she finally regained her balance, Bobbi staggered off

in the opposite direction. Gun in hand, she took it upon herself to inspect the building and ensure it was clear of infection. Halfway through, she remembered Sebastian and headed toward Andrea's room.

Inside, she found the poor animal pacing like a caged tiger. It looked both scared and confused, which wasn't surprising. Its sensitive ears must've picked up every single scream, shout, cry, growl, and snarl that echoed through the building, including the shot that ended Andrea's life.

"I'm sorry, Sebastian. Your mama's gone now, but I'll look after you," Bobbi said, holding out both arms.

For a brief moment, Sebastian didn't move. He stared at her with grass-green eyes. Finally, he walked toward her with a plaintive meow. It was almost as if he sensed the loss of Andrea and already mourned her.

Bobbi reached out to take him in her arms, and he allowed her to hold him. It seemed he'd decided to trust her. As the minutes ticked by, affection for the orphaned feline filled her heart. While nothing could ever replace her dogs, Sebastian needed her, and that was enough for her.

Chapter 6 - Robert

Robert ran toward the kitchen and grabbed the first-aid kit from the cupboard. Mason and Leo were right behind him, supporting the faltering George on either side. Susan rushed to clear the table, and they laid the injured man down on the flat surface.

"Stay strong, George," Susan said before she grabbed the kettle and put it on to boil. "We're right here beside you."

Amelia ran in with an armful of clean towels and put them to one side. "Is that enough, Robert?"

"That's perfect, honey," he replied, kissing her forehead. "Now, go back to the dorm room."

"What? No, I can help," Amelia protested.

"You mustn't see this. It'll get ugly," Robert said with a firm shake of the head.

"But—"

"Go," Robert said, waving her off.

With a quick nod, she left the room, and Robert surveyed the preparations. Things were moving fast. Sarah had the kettle boiling and a pile of rags and cleaning products readied for the aftermath of the amputation.

Removing the belt from his waist, he wrapped it around George's upper arm and tightened it. It would slow the spread of the virus and numb some of the sensation in the arm. Or so he hoped.

With the rough tourniquet in place, he asked, "You okay, buddy?"

"I'm just dandy," a pale-looking George replied.

At that moment, Rick showed up with a bottle of liquor, and a look of relief filled George's face. "Thank God."

"Here you go," Rick said, feeding the amber liquid to George straight from the bottle.

Robert placed a couple of towels underneath the operation site to absorb the blood and another rolled-up towel underneath George's head for support.

Suddenly, a shot rang out, and everybody jumped.

"What the hell was that?" Susan cried.

"It's Bobbi," Theresa said, her expression somber. "I asked her to take care of Andrea."

"I see," Robert said, and sadness filled his heart. *That's another one.*

At that moment, Clare and Frank barged into the kitchen with wild looks. "What's going on?"

"Bobbi shot Andrea before she could reanimate," Theresa explained. "And we're about to amputate George's arm. He got bitten."

"What can we do?" Frank asked.

"You can search the station for more infected," Robert said. "Take Mason and Rick with you. After that, you can check on the people next door and reassure them. Tell them everything's under control."

"Alright," Frank said, turning to Sarah. "Please stand watch on the roof. We don't know what all this noise might attract, and you're a good shot."

"I'll fetch my rifle," Sarah said.

"Ellen, please make sure Amelia and Bobbi are alright," Robert added. "That damned cat of Andrea's too."

"Okay," Ellen said with a quick nod.

"What about us?" Elijah asked, pointing from him to Benjamin and Timothy.

"Take care of the bodies and clean up the mess," Robert said.

"Alright, we're on it," Elijah said, and the kitchen emptied as everyone moved off to fulfill their duties.

Everyone rushed off, and Theresa gave George a shot in the arm. "This should take the edge off. I'm sorry I can't put you in dreamland."

Half-drunk, George managed a crooked smile. "You and me both, sister."

"What did you give him?" Mike asked.

"Morphine. The maximum dose," Theresa said.

"Don't you have local anesthetic?" Mike asked.

"We don't carry that," Theresa said, "and it wouldn't work for an amputation anyway."

"Alright. Let's do this," Ruby said, picking up a scalpel. "Hold him down."

Robert, Leo, and Mike took up their positions while Theresa set up an IV bag filled with fluids in George's other arm and placed a wad of cloth between his teeth.

"Here should do it," Ruby said, indicating a spot halfway between the elbow and bite mark. "It'll leave at least five centimeters of the ulna. Enough for proper elbow flexion."

With a wad of gauze, she disinfected the site and pressed the scalpel to George's arm. The skin split beneath the razor-sharp edge, and blood welled up from the cut. George grunted with pain, but she didn't hesitate. With a swift move, she sliced through the skin, creating two skin flaps on either side. They'd be used to cover the stump and exposed tissue after the operation.

George stiffened, and his cheeks became pale, but he didn't move. Pained grunts escaped his lips, and his throat swelled with the added pressure.

Next, Ruby severed the muscles, and blood poured from the wound in a steady stream. The thick viscous liquid pooled onto the towels below, staining them a rich crimson.

Unable to hold back, George screamed. His teeth clenched around the wad of cloth in his mouth, and his back arched off the table. Leo and Mike were taken by surprise when he tried to jerk free from their grip. They strained to hold him down, and Robert found himself fighting to keep George's arm from moving.

"Damn it! This is harder than it looks," Robert said.

"Hold him down, guys!" Ruby cried, stopping mid-cut. "I can't operate like this."

"Sorry," Robert said, pressing down with all his strength.

"Let me help," Susan said, throwing her body across George's chest. With her added weight, Robert and the others managed to get him under control.

"Hurry up, Ruby," Robert cried. "The sooner you get it done, the better."

Ruby didn't bother to reply. She resumed her grizzly task with a terse nod and sliced down to the bone. Extending the cut, she circled the radius and ulna, tied off the arteries, and resected the nerves.

The seconds ticked by as she worked, moving as fast as she dared. George fought against their hold throughout the process. His cries reverberated through the kitchen, each grizzly note a testament to his suffering.

"Can't you go any faster," he yelled, spitting out the cloth.

"Just hold on, George," Theresa said, shoving the cloth back between his teeth. "Close your eyes and think of something nice. Your best memory."

George mumbled something back but stiffened and started screaming again when Ruby resumed the operation. Finally, Ruby set the scalpel aside and held out her hand. "Saw, please."

"Here," Theresa said, handing her the tool.

Ruby sawed through the bones that tethered George's lower arm to the rest of his body. The serrated teeth grated against the hard surface, setting Robert's teeth on edge. It was a nerve-wracking sound, and he wished it would stop. *For my sake and George's.*

The pain took its toll, and George's voice grew hoarse from the screaming. Each agonized note bored into Robert's skull like a thousand knives until it felt like his skull would explode. *God, this is awful. Poor George.*

Finally, the ordeal became too much, and George fainted. He stopped fighting, slumped to the table, and he fell silent. Blessed silence fell over the room, and everyone stopped what they were doing.

After a moment, Robert cleared his throat. "Get it done, Ruby. This is your chance."

"You're right, but hold him down just in case he comes around," Ruby said. "This won't be pretty."

Using a metal file, she smoothed the rough edges of the sawed-off bone.

Leo made a choking noise. "That sound… It's like nails on a chalkboard."

"Yup," Ruby said, her lips popping on the p.

"That's just… that's just wrong," Leo said, the blood draining from his cheeks.

"You're not going to hurl, are you?" Ruby asked with a frown.

"No, I… go ahead," Leo said, turning his head to the side.

"Good," Ruby said, picking up the sutures and needle. With deft precision, she sewed together the subcutaneous tissue, closed the skin flaps, and stitched them shut. Afterward, she disinfected the site, bandaged the amputated limb, and administered a shot of antibiotics. Wiping one hand across her brow, she said, "That should do it."

Robert sighed with relief and let go of George's arm. He loosened the belt around the bicep and removed it. The poor man was still out, lying unconscious on the table, and he was glad. *At least he can't feel anything for now.*

Susan straightened up from her awkward position lying across George's chest and rubbed her lower back. "Man, that hurts. I'm not as young as I used to be. Not that it compares to George's suffering, the poor dear."

Ruby nodded. "He'll wake up soon, and he'll be in a lot of pain. We should make him as comfortable as possible."

"Where do we put him?" Robert asked. "There's no privacy in the dorm."

"He can sleep in my office," Theresa said, referring to the single bed she'd installed there the minute the world went to hell. Not only did it allow her a measure of privacy, but it also let her stay up late when she needed to work. "Besides, we need to quarantine him. Just in case."

"Good thinking. Is there a stretcher around?" Robert said, looking around.

"Over there," Ruby said, pointing with one gloved finger.

A couple of stretchers lay against the wall, left there earlier, and they loaded George onto one. It was a short walk to Theresa's office, and she went ahead to ready the space. Once they laid him down, Robert removed George's shoes, jacket, and jeans until he was dressed only in his boxers and a t-shirt.

"Thank you, Robert," Theresa said, stepping in. She wiped George's sweat-covered skin with a damp cloth and covered him with a clean sheet and blankets. Checking his temperature, she waved Robert and the rest away. "You can go. I'll watch over him."

"What if the amputation didn't work, and he turns?" Leo asked.

"I'll take care of it," Theresa said, removing a .38 Rossi from her desk drawer. "It might be small, but it'll do the job."

"Call us if you need help," Robert said.

"Of course," Theresa said, her expression bleak. "I expect an update on the situation soon. Keep me informed."

"As soon as everything has settled down, I'll be back," Robert said, waving to Leo and Mike. "Come on, guys. We have work to do."

Chapter 7 - George

When Sam's teeth sank into his flesh, George thought his number was up. There was no going back from that. It was over. He was infected, and he knew what that meant. In a few hours, he'd die and return as a soulless monster. *I'll be damned if I let that happen. I'll kill myself first.*

Sam was gone, but in his place remained the vicious evidence of his attack. The wound burned like fire, radiating heat outwards from the bite mark. Hands tugged at his shirt, and he heard someone say, "George! George, are you okay?"

He blinked, and Theresa's anxious features hovered above him. He swallowed, his mouth suddenly dry. "I got bit."

"What?" she asked.

"He bit me," George said, showing her his arm.

Theresa gasped with horror, and pulled something out of her pocket. He caught the scent of lilacs, a floral handkerchief. The kind his grandmother used to carry in her purse. It was strange because he'd never thought of Theresa as being old. Or any age. She was a force of nature. As relentless as the changing seasons.

Theresa pressed the delicate cloth to his wound, slowing the flow of blood. It hurt, but he didn't care. All that mattered was the infection radiating outward from the injury. Soon, it would enter his bloodstream, and the virus would travel to his brain. Its tentacles would take over his nervous system, waiting for him to die to seize control.

It was just a matter of time.

"George got bitten," he heard Theresa say.

"Oh, shit. What do we do?" Mason cried.

"I don't know. We must stop the bleeding and clean the wound," Theresa said. "I need a first-aid —"

"There's no time," Bobbi interrupted.

George listened to the debate as it raged above his head. When Theresa asked him what he wanted, he struggled to process the question. Cut it off? His arm? Would it even work?

A small flower of hope bloomed within his chest, and he realized one thing. If there was even the slightest chance of a cure, he wanted it. No matter the cost.

He looked from her to the gash on his arm and swallowed hard. "Do it. Just do it."

"Are you sure?" Theresa asked.

"Yes," George said, closing his eyes.

"You'd better hurry before the virus spreads," Bobbi added.

After that, George didn't hear much more. He faded in and out, probably because of the shock. Hands lifted him into the air and carried him through the air. The next moment, he was lying on the kitchen table with the light shining in his eyes.

People talked to him, and he answered. Rick fed him whiskey, and the liquor cast a hazy fuzz over his thoughts. Then Theresa jammed a needle into his arm, and the pain disappeared.

Drifting on a cloud of morphine-induced bliss, George could almost forget what had happened. There was a little pain. Not much. A tiny starburst in the universe. It was enough to make him grunt and stiffen in anticipation of what was to come. He knew it would be bad, and it was. It began as an intense cutting pain that grew deeper and deeper until it cut into his very bones. It sizzled through his nerve endings and took control of his body.

"Can't you go any faster?" he screamed.

"Just hold on, George," Theresa said, shoving the cloth back between his teeth. "Close your eyes and think of something nice. Your best memory."

A nice memory? She had to be joking. George tried to do as she suggested, but it was a futile effort. His past was nothing more than a tapestry of pain, poverty, and abuse. He had no good memories.

He fought against the hands that tried to hold him down and screamed until his throat was raw. When Ruby picked up the saw, he thought he would die. When that didn't happen, he wished for death. Anything was preferable to the brutal agony that had him in its grip. *Stop. Make it stop!*

Stop!

Stop!

Stop!

Darkness enveloped his mind, sucking him into its deep embrace. The pain faded to a distant throb, and he sank into the furthest recesses of his brain. It was safe there. It was a place where nothing could reach him. Not the infection, not the amputation, and not his memories. Then, he saw her, and an icy hand clawed at his heart.

No. Not her.

Please, not her.

But no matter how hard he tried to block out the memory, it refused to go away. Her face appeared before him, as real as the last time he saw her.

Nikki.

The air around her face solidified as the scene became clear: The threadbare carpet and faded curtains of her room—the patched dusty pink comforter on her bed. A one-eyed teddy bear called Sparky.

It wasn't a nice room. The carpet was stained, and the paint peeled from the walls. When it rained, the roof leaked in a dozen places, and the basement was a health hazard filled with mold. The air reeked of stale tobacco and cheap alcohol. An aroma that permeated every part of the run-down house on the wrong side of the tracks.

Hell, George had called it. A living hell run by a man worse than the devil. A man who had custody of George and his sister Nikki after marrying their mother. It wasn't long before she disappeared. The police thought she'd run away, but George always suspected she was dead. Buried in a shallow grave somewhere, murdered by the monster who was her husband: Rex Fisher.

The mere mention of the name was enough to send George into paroxysms of rage. He wanted to smash his fists into the man's face whenever he saw him. He wanted to scream and rail at the universe because of the sheer injustice, but he didn't. He couldn't.

Not when Rex controlled their lives. As minors, they had no say. He was their legal guardian, and that was that. Plus, the threat of them ending up in foster care was real, and George couldn't let that happen. So, he kept his mouth shut, took the abuse Rex handed out, and waited for his eighteenth birthday. When the day came, he was ready to leave except for one problem: Nikki.

"I have to leave, Sis. You know that. If I stay, he'll kill me," George said, his expression earnest.

"What do you think he'll do to me once you leave?" Nikki said.

"He's never laid a hand on you," George said.

"Because you're always in the way, but once you're gone…."

"He wouldn't dare touch you. I've notified social services. If he sets one foot wrong, they'll pounce," George said.

"You involved social services?" Nikki cried. "What if they take me away? I'll end up in the system."

"They won't. Not unless he tries something, and if that happens, you call me," George said, handing her a telephone number. "You're the only one with the number."

Nikki stared at the slip of paper, tears brimming. "I can't believe you're leaving me."

"I don't want to leave you, but I can't stay," George said, the weight of his guilt lying heavy on his shoulders.

"Then take me with you," Nikki pleaded, wringing her hands.

"He won't let me. Not until you're eighteen," George said. "He'll send the police after us."

"We'll run. We'll disappear until it's too late," Nikki said with desperate hope.

"You know it doesn't work like that. We have no money, no family, and nowhere to go. How will we find jobs? What will we eat?"

"I don't know, and I don't care," Nikki yelled, the tears spilling onto her cheeks.

"I do. I can't stand to see you starving and cold," George said.

"Then stay until I turn eighteen," Nikki insisted. "We can leave together. Build a new life far away from him."

"Don't you get it? I can't!" George shouted, his guilt causing him to lash out. "If I stay, he'll kill me, or I'll kill him. It's that simple."

"Please, don't leave, George. Please," Nikki begged. She grabbed his arm and hung on, even when he tried to pull away. "You're all I have left. Please!"

"I'm sorry, Sis. I'll come back for you. I promise," George said, backing away.

"No, you can't leave," Nikki screamed, refusing to let go of his arm. "I won't let you!"

"I'll come back when you're eighteen. I'll come back for you, I swear," George said, yanking free from her grip.

"Like you swore we'd always be together? After mom left us?" Nikki said, pointing a finger at him.

"I know, and I'm sorry, but I've got no choice," George said.

"You always have a choice," Nikki said.

"No, I —"

"You're choosing to abandon me. You're just like mom," Nikki added, her voice bitter.

"No, I'm not abandoning you," George protested, but deep down, he knew it was a lie. He was leaving her. Even worse, he was leaving her with Rex, knowing what the man was capable of.

"Just go," Nikki said, spitting out the words. She crumpled up the paper with his tel number and threw it at his face. "You're nothing to me. You hear me. Nothing!"

George ran. He ran through the house, onto the porch, down the steps, and jumped onto his motorbike, fleeing her accusing glare. He couldn't stand it, couldn't stand hurting her. It felt like his heart was being squeezed in a vice until it would burst—rupture from pure agony. *I'm sorry, Nikki.*

From the corner of his eye, he spotted her on the veranda,

standing at the top of the stairs. She stared at him without saying a word, her silence somehow worse than anything she'd said or done before.

He started the bike, revved the engine, and pulled away in a cloud of dust. As he raced down the street, she remained in his rearview mirror, a forlorn figure standing on a porch. Abandoned and alone.

The memory faded, and George flailed about in a tangle of guilt, loss, and sadness. That day was the worst of his life. It was the day he'd betrayed the only person in the world that meant something to him. The only person he'd ever loved. Worst of all, he did it because of a selfish desire for freedom.

Because she'd been right. He could've waited or taken her with him. They would've been alright, but the truth was, he didn't want to. He'd wanted to experience life alone without his little sister holding him back.

As it turned out, life without her wasn't that great either. He'd drifted for a couple of years before he became a firefighter. After that, he floated from one station to the next before settling in at the Burlington firehouse. He'd made friends and put down tentative roots there, but it never felt right. *I need her. I need Nikki.*

Time passed, and Nikki never called. The phone he'd bought remained silent, though he kept it fully charged and on him at all times. He tried phoning her, but she never answered. Each time, he left a message telling her where he was and that he loved her. He hoped she'd forgive him, but still, she never phoned. Never contacted him.

His promise to return always loomed large in his mind. What terrified him was the thought that she might reject him. That she'd throw his offer back in his face. Now, it was too late.

The apocalypse had begun, and she was lost to him.

When the zombies rose, he'd tried to call again, praying she would answer. It just rang and rang. He kept trying, however, not letting go of hope. Eventually, it stopped ringing as the lines went down, leaving him with nothing but silence: Silence and empty regrets.

Even then, he didn't give up, making quiet plans to rescue her as soon as he could make the trip. He'd ask Theresa for a vehicle and supplies once everything at the station had settled down.

Now that dream was gone. He'd never make it with only one arm; even if he could, chances were she was dead already—a zombie.

It was time to face the facts. Nikki was lost to him, and he had no one to blame but himself. If he hadn't left her, she'd still be alive. They'd be together, facing the world as one. Just like they'd faced Rex in the past. As a unit. Brother and sister. *I'm sorry, Nikki. I hope wherever you are, you can forgive me because I'll never forgive myself.*

Chapter 8 - Amelia

After she left the kitchen, Amelia made her way back to the dorm room. She left the scene in the kitchen with reluctance, acutely aware that she had nothing to offer. No medical experience, fighting skills, or marksmanship. She knew nothing about growing or storing food and had negligible upper body strength. *Hell, I can't even cook, clean, or sew.*

The only thing she was truly good at was accounting. Numbers were her jam, she knew how to rock a power suit, and she could put together one hell of a PowerPoint presentation. Her days consisted of store-bought coffee, high heels, countless meetings, and combing the books of floundering companies and budding entrepreneurs. None of which meant a single thing during the zombie apocalypse.

Wrapping her arms around her middle, she braved the darkened hallway. A shiver shot down her spine as she walked, and memories of the evening flashed through her mind. The sight of Donna and Sam's crazed expressions were at the forefront. A horrible scene that she never wanted to experience again.

Suddenly, a shot rang out, and Amelia froze. The sound was deafening, and her ears rang with the force of the blast. Covering both ears with her palms, she dropped to a crouch.

Hunched over, she waited for the worst to pass. Finally, her ears stopped ringing, and she straightened up. A hand fell onto her shoulder, and she screamed. "Who's there?"

"Calm down. It's just me, Frank," a voice replied.

"Jeez, don't do that." Amelia pressed one hand to her chest, trying to calm her frantically beating heart. She spied Frank in the gloom, shadowed by Clare, Rick, and Mason.

"Sorry," Frank said, though he didn't look in the least apologetic.

"What was that shot about?" she asked, looking down the hallway.

"It's Andrea," Frank said.

"Huh?" Amelia asked, confused. "But isn't she dead?"

"She is, and Theresa asked Bobbi to take care of her should she…." Frank hesitated.

"Should she what?" Amelia said.

"Should she decide not to be dead anymore," Clare added.

"Oh, I see," Amelia said as realization dawned. Feeling dumb, she shrugged. "I didn't think of that, sorry."

"That's okay," Clare said with a brittle smile. It didn't sit well on her face and revealed how tense she was.

Amelia did not find that surprising. It had been a tough night for all of them, and even the toughest among the group showed the effects. *We have to keep it together.* "Where are you lot going?"

"We're searching the place to ensure there's no more danger. No more infected," Mason explained, brandishing his gun.

"Can I come with you?" Amelia asked.

"No," Frank said. "You're not armed."

"But—"

"Sorry," he said, his expression firm.

Amelia's shoulders drooped. Sitting alone in the dorm room frightened her, and she felt vulnerable.

"We'll take you as far as the dorm, okay?" Frank added.

"Okay," she replied.

"Stay close," he said, taking the lead. Amelia fell in line behind him and the armed Clare, Rick, and Mason, glad to have the company. The fire station appeared dark and threatening now. It was no longer the haven of before.

They walked through the narrow corridor with Frank inspecting every room they came across. There was the men's bathroom, locker room, a supply closet, an empty office turned into a makeshift pantry, and the men's dorm room. They were all empty with no signs of life. Neither dead nor alive.

As they turned a corner, they spotted Andrea's body. She still lay where she'd fallen, a broken doll covered in blood. The only difference was the bullet hole in her forehead.

Frank briefly inspected the corpse before he moved on. Amelia skirted around the dead woman, staring at her face. It didn't look like Andrea anymore. What remained was nothing more than an empty vessel devoid of the spirit that used to animate it. *One day that'll be me.*

She tried to push the morbid thought aside and focused on the path ahead. It wasn't long before they reached the women's dorm room, and Frank waved at the door. "This is your stop."

"Are you sure I can't come with you?" Amelia pleaded.

"It's too dangerous," Frank said, shaking his head. "After the station, we're checking the street outside and the people next door. It'll be better if you stay here."

"Fine," Amelia said, resigned to her fate.

Frank and the others left, continuing on their way. Amelia closed the door with a sigh and turned around. With her back pressed to the door, she surveyed the room. It was dark and, after everything, scary. The darkness seemed to breathe. It was a living creature waiting to pounce, and her heart pounded with fear. "Oh, hell no!"

Hurrying toward the bed, Amelia switched on the lamp. Golden light flooded her cubicle and formed a warm halo around the area. It chased away the feeling of dread that threatened to suck the life from her soul, but it couldn't dispel the knowledge that she was useless. Superfluous. A burden to her husband and everyone charged with protecting her life.

Suddenly the dorm room's door opened, and a bright blonde head appeared silhouetted in the light. "Amelia? Are you there?"

Amelia perked up. "Ellen?"

"That's me," Ellen said. "Robert asked me to check up on you and Bobbi. Andrea's cat, too."

"He did?" Amelia said, love for her husband filling her heart. A good man and a wonderful husband, he never failed to amaze her with his consideration and care.

"Yup. He did," Ellen said. "So? How are you holding up?"

"Not great, actually," Amelia admitted.

"I don't blame you," Ellen said, walking into the room. She took a seat next to Amelia on the bed. "It's been a trippy evening."

"Trippy isn't quite how I'd describe it," Amelia said.

"No, I suppose not," Ellen said.

"I just feel so useless," Amelia exclaimed.

"Why would you feel like that?" Ellen asked. "You are the furthest thing from useless that I can think of."

"I can't do anything. I can't shoot, fight, or even cook. I'm not domestic or even very fit. I'm only slim because I live on

55

caffeine and adrenalin most of the time."

Ellen laughed. "That's not true, and you know it. You're a survivor."

"Am I? Robert had to save me from my own office block."

"Sure he did, and in saving you, you saved him," Ellen pointed out.

"What?"

"Don't you see? You're his heart, Amelia. Without you, Robert can't function. He'll always need you to steer him right."

"Do you think so?" Amelia asked.

"I know so," Ellen said with a decisive nod. "Besides, whining and moping about never helped anyone."

Amelia choked on a laugh. "Did you just call me whiny?"

Ellen winked. "Maybe a little bit."

"Thanks. I needed to hear that, and you're right," Amelia said. "I've been feeling very sorry for myself when others lie dead or might be dying."

"Well, do you feel better now?" Ellen asked.

"Much better," Amelia said, and it was true. Ellen's words had reawakened the fight inside her heart, and she felt a surge of renewed determination.

"Come on then," Ellen said with a soft smile. "Let's go check on Bobbi and… Sebastian, is it?"

"I think so," Amelia said. "Andrea showed him to me once. He's cute, but I'm allergic to cats."

"Keep your distance then," Ellen said, walking toward the door. "And afterward, we'll find something to do. That way, you won't feel quite so useless anymore."

"Deal," Amelia said, standing up. "Just let me put on some proper clothes. I'm still wearing my pajamas."

"Good idea," Ellen acknowledged. She glanced at her watch and shrugged. "It's almost dawn anyway. Nobody is going back to sleep after this."

"That's for sure," Amelia said. She made up her mind as she pulled on a set of clean clothes. *No more moping. No more whining. You can do this.*

Chapter 9 - Frank

After they escorted Amelia to her dorm room, Frank canvassed the rest of the station with Clare, Mason, and Rick in tow. They searched every nook and cranny until they were satisfied no more danger lurked within the building's confines.

Along the way, they found Bobbi looking after Sebastian and Ellen, who was on her way to check on Amelia. They also encountered Elijah, Benjamin, and Timothy in the women's bathroom, mopping up the blood and brains that stained the tiles. It was an unpleasant task, and Frank didn't envy them.

"Where are the bodies?" Frank asked, eyeing the empty hallway.

"We took them downstairs and put them in a storeroom. Donna too. We'll bury them in the morning," Elijah said with a mournful look.

Frank nodded. "We're on our way out now."

"Out?" Elijah asked.

"We need to check on the people next door. Reassure them and such. They would've heard the shots, and they must be pretty scared," Frank explained.

"Ah, good thinking," Elijah said. "Be careful out there. Who knows what else heard the commotion and came running."

"We'll be careful," Frank replied before continuing his

security check.

They bypassed the kitchen where Susan had begun the job of cleaning up after the operation. All was quiet, the amputation over.

"Poor George," Clare whispered, her eyes wide.

"You can say that again," Mason said. "He has a long road ahead of him. If he survives."

"You think he won't?" Clare asked.

"I hope he does, but infection can be a bitch, and we don't have the proper facilities to treat him," Mason said.

"Alright, guys. That's enough," Frank said. "We have a job to do."

"Sorry," Mason said, looking contrite.

"Remember what Elijah said. People aren't the only things drawn to noise. Zombies are too. Be alert and keep your eyes and ears open," Frank cautioned.

"Yes, Sir," Clare acknowledged, with Mason and Rick following her example.

They quickly searched the bay area but found nothing of interest. Donna, Sam, and Andrea lay where they'd been placed, their bodies wrapped in sheets.

Frank stared at them for a few seconds, his heart hurting with the loss. He hadn't known any of them well. Not even Donna. But they'd been good people, and their deaths weighed heavy on his shoulders. He felt responsible, as well. He was the one who'd brought Donna into the station, and he was the one who failed to pick up on her illness. *This is my fault, and so is George's injury. If only I'd been more careful.*

But empty regrets would get him nowhere, and he led the way to the weapons' locker. The door opened readily, the keys dangling in the slot. "Take what you need, everyone. Whatever gun you're most comfortable with."

"Don't mind if I do," Rick said, exchanging the pistol Clare had given him earlier for a Glock 22 and an extra magazine. He also hung an ax from his belt as a backup weapon before stepping back. "Your turn, Mason."

Mason picked up an AR-15 rifle and changed the setting to semi-automatic. He, too, added an ax to his belt and tucked a spare cartridge into his pocket. "That's me."

Frank looked at Clare. "What about you?"

"I'm good," Clare said, patting her riot shotgun with a resolute look.

With its shorter barrel and extended magazine, it packed quite a punch. She also carried a knife on both hips, an addition Frank only noticed at that moment. She looked like a fighter with her dark hair, piercing green eyes, and leather jacket. She moved like one too, and he reflected that she would've made an excellent cop.

"Alright. Are you ready?" Frank asked.

"I'm ready," Clare said.

"So am I," Mason echoed.

"Me too," Rick added.

"Your fingers won't be a problem?" Frank asked.

"Not if I can help it," Rick said.

"Alright, let's go," Frank said.

"What about the garage door?" Clare asked. "We don't know what's outside. What if we're overrun?"

"You make a good point," Frank said, kicking himself mentally for not thinking about it first. "And we can't leave the door open either. Not when we have to go next door."

"We need someone to stand guard," Mason added.

"We can do it," Robert said, his voice coming from the stairs.

With him stood Leo and Mike.

"How's George doing?" Frank asked.

"As well as can be expected," Robert said. "He's resting in Theresa's office, and she's ready should he take a turn for the worse."

"Good," Frank said. "The weapon's locker is open. We'll wait until you're all armed."

"We're on it," Robert said.

Frank waited while they were gone, shifting from one foot to the other with nervous energy. The entire night had been a disaster, and he wondered what awaited them outside the bay doors.

Elijah, Benjamin, and Timothy showed up a few minutes in. Frank quickly filled them in, and they volunteered to help.

Thinking it over, Frank made a couple of swift decisions. "Timothy, you're good with a rifle, right?"

"Yes, Sir."

"Grab a gun and join Sarah on the roof. You can cover us from there and let us know if you see trouble coming. Take a radio with you," Frank said. He went to the equipment rack and chose a couple of portable radios. Handing one to Timothy, he clipped the other to his belt.

"Will do, Sir," Timothy said, grabbing a rifle and taking the radio. He disappeared up the stairs, and Frank waved to Leo. "You come with us. The rest of you defend the station."

"Good luck," Robert said, forming a defensive line next to Elijah, Benjamin, and Mike.

Frank felt his insides warm with approval. While Robert and his colleagues weren't trained officers, they were no cowards either, ready to lay down their lives for their fellow man. *I couldn't have asked for better company during the apocalypse.*

After a few minutes, the radio at his belt crackled.

"Sir? It's Timothy."

"Yes?" Frank answered.

"It's clear outside. No zombies."

"Are you sure?"

"We're sure, Sir."

"Alright, thanks, kid," Frank said. He turned toward the bay doors and signaled to Robert. "Open up."

Robert pushed the remote button, and the doors lifted slowly. The hinges creaked, the sound sharp in the predawn air. Chill air rushed inside, ruffling Frank's collar, and a shiver ran down his spine. Ready for action, he waited.

The bay doors rattled to a halt, the exit wide open. Outside, the street was empty, and not a creature stirred. It was still dark, but a faint lightening on the horizon heralded the coming dawn. Soon, the sun would shine on a new day. *Let's hope it's a better one.*

Chapter 10 - Ellen

Ellen left the dorm room with Amelia in tow. She looked from one end of the hall to the other, unsure where to begin. "Do you know where Bobbi is?"

"No, I haven't seen her," Amelia said.

"I suppose we could check on the cat, er… Sebastian first. Make sure it's okay," Ellen said. "Then we can look for Bobbi."

"Go ahead. I'm right behind you," Amelia said.

Together, they headed toward the office where Andrea used to sleep. Recently, it had been dubbed the coms room. Coms being short for communications. Andrea had acted as their go-between, spending hours trawling the radio waves looking for survivors. Now that she was gone, they'd need somebody else to take over her job. *What about her cat? Sebastian? Who'll look after it now?*

There were no ready answers to those questions, and Ellen pushed them aside. They'd cross that bridge when they got to it. For the moment, they had more pressing concerns. Things such as the safety of everything they held dear.

The problem was that she didn't know quite where to start. The only thing she could think of was checking in on the cat. After all, taking care of a defenseless animal was a good deed and might balance out some of the bad that had happened that night.

When they reached the coms room, Ellen cracked open the door and peeked inside. To her surprise, she spotted Bobbi sitting on the sofa with Sebastian curled up on her lap. Soft music played in the background, and the atmosphere was one of peace and quiet.

"Err, sorry to bother you. I'm just here to check on you and Sebastian," Ellen said, feeling like an intruder.

"Who wants to know?" Bobbi asked.

"Robert sent me."

"Pfft, Robert. As if he really cares about Sebastian," Bobbi scoffed.

Sebastian meowed as if in agreement, a distinct growl in the mix.

"It's not just him. We all care," Ellen said, a touch defensive.

"Well, as you can see, we're doing just fine," Bobbi said in a curt tone of voice. "Right, Sebastian?"

Sebastian stared at Ellen with slitted green eyes, its whiskers twitching with annoyance. It clearly didn't welcome the intrusion, and its message was clear. *Get out.*

"Thanks for checking up on us, and you can tell Robert we're fine," Bobbi added.

"Okay. I'll leave you to it then," Ellen said, flushing bright red. She pulled back but paused. "I really was worried about you. So was Amelia."

Amelia waved at Bobbi from the hallway. "Hi, Bobbi. Sebastian."

Bobbi stared at them for a few seconds before she sighed. "I'm sorry. I didn't mean to be rude. It's been a long night."

"That it has," Ellen agreed. "Do you need anything?"

"No, thank you. I'll stay with Sebastian for now. He needs the company," Bobbi said. "I'll listen out for any communications on the radio too."

"Sounds good. I'll bring you something to eat and drink once everything has settled down," Ellen said. "It's almost time for breakfast, right?"

"I'd appreciate that," Bobbi said with a faint smile.

Closing the door, Ellen looked at Amelia. "I guess they're okay for now."

"I guess so," Amelia said with a shrug. "What now?"

"Let's check up on the rest. See where we're needed," Ellen suggested. "There's no point in going to bed. I'd never be able to sleep anyway."

"Good thinking," Amelia said, and they continued down the hallway, where they found Elijah, Benjamin, and Timothy cleaning the blood from the walls, tiles, and carpet.

"It looks like you guys could use some help," Ellen said.

"That we do," Elijah said. "This is all that's left."

"Left?" Ellen asked.

"We wrapped the bodies in sheets, moved them downstairs to the bay area, and cleaned up the mess down there." Elijah pulled a face. "It wasn't pretty."

"So it's just this?" Ellen asked, waving a hand across the scene.

"If you can call it just this," Elijah said. "There's blood and brains all over the show."

"Squeamish, Elijah?" Ellen teased.

"Me? What about you?"

"I slaughtered my first chicken when I was six. My first pig at eight. By the time I was twelve, I'd shot, skinned, and butchered my first buck," Ellen said. When everyone stared at her like she'd grown two heads, she clarified. "I grew up on a farm. So no. I'm not squeamish."

Elijah tossed her a damp rag and grinned. "Put your money where your mouth is."

"Happy to," Ellen said, grabbing a bottle of bleach and a bucket.

"I'll help, too," Amelia said, picking up a mop.

"More hands make for light work, as my mom used to say," Timothy quipped.

"Your mom was right," Ellen said with a wry smile. "And my mom used to say the exact same thing."

"Clever ladies," Amelia said.

"Let's get to it then," Elijah said, handing out sets of gloves. "Glove up, everyone. We don't want to take any chances."

"Thanks," Ellen said, pulling on the gloves. She got down on her hands and knees, scrubbing the blood-stained carpet. Bits and pieces of bone, tissue, and other unmentionable matter found their way into a plastic bag, and it wasn't long before the water in the bucket had turned a hideous rust red.

Amelia didn't take it quite so well. Her cheeks turned pale, and more than once, she had to take a few seconds to compose herself. Even so, they made quick work of the mess between the five of them.

After cleaning the area, they disinfected the site, threw the contaminated material into a plastic bag for removal, and returned the supplies to the storeroom.

There was nothing to be done about the hideous stains on the carpet, however, short of replacing it. Not even bleach could get it out. The powerful detergent merely served to add its own distinct yellowish color to the mix, forming an eyesore that no amount of trying could wish away.

"I suppose we could throw a rug over it," Amelia said, eyeing the ugly blotches.

"If we can find one," Ellen agreed, turning to Elijah. "What about you guys? What's next on the list?"

"We'll check on the others. Frank and his group are inspecting the building before they go out. Maybe, they'll need our help."

"Go ahead," Ellen said. "I think we'll check on George."

Elijah nodded. "I hope he's okay."

"Well, he stopped screaming a few minutes ago," Benjamin said, referring to a sound they'd all tried to ignore while they were busy cleaning. "That must mean something."

"Yeah, but is it something good or something bad?" Elijah said, and a troubled silence filled the hall.

Clearing her throat, Ellen broke the stalemate. "Anyway, you guys check on Frank's group, and we'll visit George."

"Deal," Elijah said, hurrying away with Benjamin and Timothy close on his heels.

"I hope George is alright," Ellen said as she and Amelia walked to the kitchen.

"I hope so, too," Amelia said. "Robert didn't want me to see it."

"He was right. It's an ugly business," Ellen said. "Seeing someone in pain like that."

"Have you seen a lot of it? That sort of thing?" Amelia said.

"Live amputations? Thank God, no. But I've seen plenty of nasty stuff on calls. Burnt flesh is the worst," Ellen said with a shudder. "The smell... sometimes I have nightmares about it."

Amelia folded her arms around her middle and hugged herself close. "I can't imagine."

"Pray you never experience it," Ellen said.

Moments later, they entered the kitchen to find it empty

except for Susan. The woman was busy mopping the floor, and the smell of bleach and disinfectant hung thick in the air. She spotted Ellen and Amelia and waved them over. "You're just in time."

"Just in time for what?" Ellen asked.

"Time to help me prepare breakfast," Susan said.

"Breakfast?" Ellen said, glancing at her watch. "Isn't it a bit early? It's just after four."

"By the time everyone comes back from their tasks, they'll be cold, tired, and hungry. The least we can do is offer them something warm to eat and drink. Agreed?" Susan said, hands on her hips.

"Agreed," Ellen said, pulling up her sleeves. "Are you in, Amelia?"

"Of course," Amelia said. "I'll get started on the coffee."

"Thank you," Susan said, picking up a bucket of dirty water and a bag full of bloody towels. "I'll take care of this and come back for the arm." With those words, Susan strode out of the kitchen, leaving behind a shocked and bemused audience.

Ellen stared at her retreating back. "Did she say arm?"

"As in George's arm?" Amelia said.

Ellen turned toward the kitchen table and spotted an object wrapped in plastic. It looked suspiciously like an arm, and she swallowed hard on the sudden knot in her throat. "Is that…?"

"I think so," Amelia said, one hand pressed to her mouth.

"I don't think I'm hungry anymore," Ellen said, whirling around.

"Me neither," Amelia said, her skin tinged with green.

"Oh, come on, girls. It's not that bad," Susan said, reentering the kitchen. She picked up the arm and cradled it in both hands. "Show some respect. This used to be part of George once."

"We know," Ellen said, her stomach taking a turn. "That's the problem."

"Alright, alright," Susan said with a grin. "I'll take it away if you promise to get started on the food."

"We promise," Ellen said, waving her away.

Susan left, much to the relief of Ellen and Amalia. Sharing an amused look, they turned to the task of feeding a station full of hungry people.

"Let's see. What have we got?" Ellen said, opening the fridge. "Ooh, there's eggs."

"Eggs?" Amelia said. "I thought we were out?"

"We were until Robert raided that supermarket two blocks over. The eggs were still good. They can last a while outside the fridge, especially with cold weather like this," Ellen said. "A lot of things are still good. Not the milk and bread, though."

"I'm going to miss fresh milk," Amelia said, putting on a pot of coffee.

"Me too. Maybe we should get a cow. Keep her in the garage next to the trucks," Ellen said with a laugh.

"How about the roof? At least she'll get some fresh air up there," Amelia quipped.

"If we can get her up the stairs," Ellen said.

"Hey, girls. I'm back, minus the arm," Susan said, greeting them with a smile. "Have we decided what to make for breakfast yet?"

"How about scrambled eggs?" Ellen asked.

"With what?" Susan asked, cocking her head.

"There's onions, tomatoes, and ham," Ellen said. "How about a veggie egg scramble?"

"Like a frittata?" Susan asked.

"Er, sure. If that's what it's called," Ellen said.

"You don't?"

"No, my mom used to call it mishmash eggs or mengelmoes in Afrikaans," Ellen said.

"Meng…il…muss… what?" Susan said, trying to pronounce the foreign word.

"Yeah, I'm not even going to attempt that one," Amelia said with a laugh.

"Mishmash eggs it is," Ellen announced.

"Just that? We don't have bread, and I'm not in the mood to bake," Susan said.

"Pancakes and syrup?" Amelia offered.

"Sounds good," Susan said with an approving nod. "Let's get cracking."

"I'll start on the batter," Amelia said.

"I'll whip the eggs," Susan said.

"And I'll do the chopping," Ellen said, grabbing an armful of onions, tomatoes, and ham. With a knife in hand, she began her preparations.

As she sliced, diced, and quartered, she thought back to when she was a little girl, learning how to cook under her mom's tutelage. Back then, she wasn't a firefighter, or a zombie killer, or anything special at all. She was just a kid learning how to bake her first cookie and fry her first egg.

"Do you miss it?" Amelia asked. "Your home, I mean."

"I miss the way the sun rose over the veldt, and the smell of moer koffie early in the morning," Ellen said.

"What's moer koffie?" Amelia asked.

"It's like filter coffee but better," Ellen said. "I don't know how to explain it, but there's nothing like it on earth. I used to sit on the verandah and watch the sunrise with a cup of coffee in one hand and a buttermilk rusk in the other. Rusks are like biscuits. You dunk them in your coffee before you eat them."

"That sounds so yummy," Amelia said.

Ellen shrugged. "There are many things I miss about my home: The farm, my family, the animals, and the smell of rain hitting the dirt. I just hope they're okay and that they're weathering the storm."

"I'm sure they are," Susan said with a sympathetic look. "From what you've told me in the past, your family is strong and resourceful. They'll survive."

"Maybe, but I won't be there to see it," Ellen said. "I'll never get to see them again."

"I'm sorry, dear. If it's any consolation, you're like family to me," Susan said.

"And me," Amelia added.

"Thanks," Ellen said, but it wasn't the same.

In her mind, she pictured her father, tanned, broad-shouldered, dressed in khakis, and carrying a rifle. Her twin brothers were younger versions of him, already schooled in the ways of the farm. They could tell by a single look if one of the sheep was sick and had spent many a night catching lambs during the breeding season.

Her mother worked in the home, but she was no doormat. With one look, she could quell a rising argument around the dinner table and set someone straight if they were being disrespectful. She was the family matriarch and ruled her domain with an iron fist. Yet, never had a kinder person set foot on the earth, and she spent many an evening knitting blankets and readying food parcels for the poor.

Even when Ellen rebelled against farm life, they supported her. After school, they paid for her to attend a college in Cape

Town, and when she decided to work abroad, they cheered her on.

With a shake of the head, she tried to dismiss the memories. They were best left for quiet moments in the middle of the night. Then she could mourn their loss without upsetting her friends. Besides, she wasn't the only one missing her family. Everyone had someone they cared about, like Susan's son Noah. *At least my family is still alive. Noah too. Not everyone is that lucky, and it does no good to complain. Maybe one day, I'll see them again.*

Chapter 11 - Mason

Mason stepped out into the cold and looked up and down the road. All was quiet, and no sound could be heard in the hushed atmosphere. No snarling, growling, or shuffling. No footsteps, either dragging or running, could be heard. All was quiet except for the wind whistling through the alleyway, scattering a carpet of dried leaves.

The streetlamp next to him cast a circle of orange light on the pavement, creating a halo effect around him. It struck him as funny because he was no angel and never had been. While he considered himself a good guy, he wasn't a saint and didn't believe in anything he couldn't see or touch.

"Doesn't look like any infected got in," Clare said, joining him.

"I wouldn't be so sure of that," Mason replied. "They can be sneaky bastards."

"True. I'll keep my eyes peeled," she said.

"Come on, guys," Frank said. "Look alive."

"Do all old policemen talk like that?" Clare whispered. "Look alive. Be alert. Blah-blah-blah."

Mason stifled a snort. "Shut up, Sis. You'll get us into trouble."

"I'm just joking," Clare said with a grin. "You know me."

"Exactly, I know you, and you always manage to put your foot in it," Mason said, chucking her on the shoulder.

"Whatever," she said, rolling her eyes.

They followed Frank to the building next door and up the steps toward the entrance. A dim light shone around the edges of the door, and muffled voices sounded from the inside. They were arguing, and Mason could make out some of the words.

"We can't just stand here. We have to do something," one voice said.

"You want… out there? … too dangerous!" another replied. "… be a such… coward."

"Not… Think of the children. Their protection… priority."

"Well, I'm going to find out… going on. Out of my way."

"Seems like we're just in time," Frank said, banging on the security gate with one fist. "Hello? Anybody in there?"

The voices went silent for a few seconds before someone called out. A woman. "Who's there?"

"It's Officer Frank Hearn from next door," Frank said. "We've come to talk to you about what happened earlier."

"Hold on," the voice said.

The door opened, and a woman appeared inside the frame. She wore a thick polo neck jersey with jeans, and her graying hair was drawn back into a loose knot. Dark bags lined her eyes, and she looked almost as tired as she probably was. She also looked cranky as hell, and Mason knew she'd be trouble.

"I'm sorry to bother you at this hour, ma'am, but a lot has happened, and we wanted to reassure you," Frank said.

"Well, it's about time," the woman exclaimed. "We've been worried sick. First, there were the screams, then the gunshot, then more screaming. We thought it was the end. What in God's name is going on?"

74

"Yes, I know, and I apologize," Frank said.

"Apology not accepted. What's going on?"

"We had an outbreak inside the fire station."

"An outbreak?" the woman said with a gasp. She pressed one hand to her chest, visibly shaken. "Has it been contained? Do we need to leave?"

"Nobody is going anywhere. You are quite safe, I assure you," Frank said, his tone soothing. "The outbreak was contained, and the affected parties neutralized."

"Neutralized? You mean killed?" the woman repeated.

"Yes, unfortunately, we had no choice," Frank said.

"How did the infection get in? This is supposed to be a safe place. You promised," the woman cried, her voice becoming strident.

Before Frank could reply, another woman stepped in. Mason recognized her as one of the teachers they'd rescued from the school called Sandi. She had soft brown hair and kind eyes, but her voice was firm when she said, "Claudia, please calm down. You'll frighten the children."

"The children? They're already frightened," Claudia said, but she lowered her tone to a fierce whisper. "I want to know what's going on, and I want to know now."

"Look, ma'am," Frank said. "Everything will be explained in good time, but please go back to your beds for now. You are safe; trust me."

"Trust you? I'm sorry, but that's not good enough," Claudia said, folding her arms.

Before the situation could escalate any further, Sandi said. "Officer Hearn. Will there be a meeting of some sort tomorrow?"

"A meeting?" Frank asked, perplexed.

"About the err... events tonight?" she added.

"I suppose we could arrange something."

"Excellent. If you could let us know what time, we'll gladly attend, and we can straighten out this whole misunderstanding," Sandi said. "Right, Claudia?"

Caught off guard, Claudia stuttered, "Um, sure. Whatever."

"I'll see what we can do," Frank said, visibly relieved. "For now, the best thing to do would be to get some rest. Everything is fine."

"Thank you, Officer," Sandi said, ushering Claudia away from the door. "I'm sure you have much to do, so we'll leave you to it. Good night, and thank you for stopping by to allay our fears."

"It's our pleasure, ma'am," Frank said with a polite nod. "Good night, ladies."

Sandi closed the door, shutting them out, and the sound of retreating footsteps could be heard on the other side of the door.

Mason blew out a breath. "Oowee, that's one tough cookie."

"Claudia? I thought she was a bitch," Clare said.

"Oh, she is," Mason said as they walked again. "I was talking about Sandi."

"Sandi?" Clare said with a frown. "Is that the other woman's name?"

"Yes, if I'm not mistaken, she's a teacher and a lot tougher than she looks."

"Do I detect a hint of admiration, Bro?" Clare asked with a teasing smile. "I thought you had the hots for Sarah."

"I don't have the hots for anyone," Mason protested.

"You mooned over her at the party."

"I did not!"

"Did too."

"Did not.

"Don't make me come back there," Frank said, waving a finger at them. "You're not too old for a hiding. Both of you."

"Corporal punishment is a crime," Clare said.

"Not anymore," Frank said with a wicked grin. "It's the apocalypse. No rules, right?"

"Spoilsport," Clare grumbled.

"Just shut up and keep your eyes peeled for trouble," Frank said. "We're doing a circuit of the block, then heading back."

Together, they walked up the street and inspected every dark alleyway, nook, and cranny. Periodically, Frank would check in with Timothy, but all remained quiet. Even the barricades were silent, though they spotted a couple of wandering zombies beyond the barriers.

To Mason, it meant the infected were still very much around, but the barricades were doing their jobs. It also appeared that a single distant gunshot and some screaming wasn't enough to draw them en masse. That didn't mean other people wouldn't notice, however. A fact Frank mentioned on their way back to the station.

"While I've got you lot here with me, I want to talk to you about something that you might not realize, but Leo and I know for a fact," Frank said.

"What's that?" Mason asked.

"Zombies aren't your only enemies out here," Frank said. "Other people are just as dangerous, if not more so. Now that law and order are gone, and no one is left to enforce it, chaos rules."

"He's right. As police officers, we've seen what people can do, and it's a lot worse than anything the zombies will do to you," Leo said.

"So, remember. People can't be trusted. Not at first. They're as likely to kill you as the zombies are," Frank said. "Even seemingly good people."

"What do you mean?" Mason asked.

"Picture this. You meet a woman with three kids. They're on the run and starving when you meet them. You think you can trust her because she looks okay. Just a mom, right?" Frank asked.

"Right," Mason said.

"Wrong. She's probably the most dangerous person you could meet out on the road because if it comes down to keeping her kids alive, she'll do anything. Literally, anything, and that includes killing you and taking what you have. Understand?" Frank asked.

"What you're saying is, it's not just the obvious criminal types we have to look out for," Mason said. "Anyone could be a threat."

"Exactly, and the longer this apocalypse carries on, the worse it will get. People will start to lose their humanity after a while. If you spend enough time hunting, killing, and surviving, all the rules and inhibitions of the before will fall away. We'll revert to what we were thousands of years before. Savage beasts."

"You think that'll happen to us?" Mason asked.

Frank shrugged. "I hope not, but time will tell. A few years from now, you won't recognize yourself. None of us will."

Silence fell as they walked the last few steps to the station, each lost in thought. Mason couldn't help but mull over Frank's words. While much of it was common sense, some came as a revelation. *In a few years, none of us will be able to recognize ourselves. But will the change be for the better or, the worse?*

Chapter 12 - Sarah

Sarah leaned against the roof's edge and scanned the nearest barricade through the scope of her rifle. Nothing stirred, and she moved on to the next. There were four barriers in total, blocking off a neat square of buildings from the rest of the city.

Inside the block lay the fire station, the import and export warehouse, the office block next door, the gas station, the clinic, a small supermarket, and a few other buildings. They had cleared all during the past few weeks. It was a small island of humanity amid a town overrun with zombies.

She had to admit that the idea was genius, and though it wasn't perfect, it was home. They now needed to build on the foundations they'd created. They could do it; she knew they could, but it saddened her too.

It saddened her because it was too late for the thousands that had already died. For the friends and family that they'd lost. Her sister. Her parents. Everyone.

Tears pricked her eyelids, the yawning pit in her heart an empty void she could never fill again. The memories of that first day returned. The death and destruction at the precinct, their narrow escape, looking for their family and friends in the hours and days after that. Only to meet with failure.

Sarah closed her eyes, vividly remembering the scene at her parent's house. It wasn't something she wanted to relive, but it was impossible to resist. She kept picking at the scabs on the wound, keeping the pain alive in her heart. It was a form of punishment, she supposed—a way to pay for surviving when everyone she loved was dead.

***

Sarah climbed out of Leo's police car, her stomach a churning pit of anxiety. Her sister Anne's car stood in the driveway, parked behind her father's old Mercedes. The driver's door stood open, and a trail of blood led toward the front door.

A crimson handprint was smeared across the pane of glass that abutted the heavy wooden door, and the entrance yawned open to all comers.

"Are you sure you want to go in there?" Leo asked. "We can check it out for you."

"No, I'm going in," Sarah said.

"You shouldn't," Frank said. "What if they've turned?"

"Then I'll take care of it," Sarah said, lifting her chin.

"You can't," Frank protested. "It's not right. That's your family. No person should be forced to kill their own family."

"I said I'll take care of it," Sarah said, shooting him a cold glare.

Frank stared at her for a few seconds, his years of experience heavily imprinted in each line of his face. Sarah supposed she should listen to him. He knew what he was talking about, but she couldn't. *That's my people in there. My blood. It's my responsibility.*

With her gun gripped in both hands, she approached the house. She went up the steps one at a time until she reached the door. There, she paused, nudging the door open with one foot.

It swung wide, and Sarah spotted a pool of blood in the foyer. She didn't know who it belonged to but prayed it wasn't Anne or her parents. The chances of a happy ending were slim, however, and she prepared herself for the worst.

Armed and ready, she moved deeper into the house. Frank followed her while Leo stood guard at the door. The trail of blood moved through the foyer and living room, into the hallway, and beyond.

"Be careful," Frank said in a low voice.

"I know," Sarah said, feeling a spurt of irritation. *I'm not a child.*

She checked the first room on her left, taking a quick turn into the room with her gun at the ready.

It was empty.

Repeating the maneuver, she cleared the next room and the next. Finally, there was only one room left. Her parents' bedroom.

The door yawned open, and she stepped inside, not knowing what to expect. The first thing she saw was blood. Blood everywhere. On the walls, the ceiling, the carpet, and the bedding. It drenched the room until it reeked of death.

Horror froze her to the spot, and ice flushed through her veins. Unable to move, she stood like that until a low growl sounded from the bowels of the room. It was soft and low. Almost feminine.

Swallowing hard, Sarah turned in the direction of the noise. She didn't want to see what it was, or who it was, but she had to look. When she realized who it was, she shook her head with sorrow. "Oh, Anne. I'm so sorry."

Her sister crouched over the bodies of their parents. Both

were dead, their bodies torn to pieces. There wasn't even enough left to reanimate. Even their skulls were cracked open like rotten eggs, killed by their eldest daughter.

Anne was unrecognizable. Barely human. Drenched in blood, her hair was matted to her skull, and her clothes the color of crimson. She bared her bloody teeth and snarled, bits of flesh clutched in her fists. With a shriek, she pounced, closing the distance fast.

Time slowed to a crawl, and everything seemed to happen in slow motion: Anne launching her body through the air. Sarah's blood pulsing through her veins. Her heartbeat thudding in her ears. Her finger tightening around the trigger.

A single breath…

Boom!

Anne collapsed to the ground.

It was over.

***

Sarah choked on a sob, the memory as fresh and painful as the moment it happened. It burned like acid, eating away at her peace. Each time she relived it, she lost a piece of her soul. *It should've been me. Anne was the better of us. She deserved to live.*

But regret was a useless emotion, and she pushed it aside. For the moment, at least. She had a job to do and couldn't afford to get distracted. People died that way, and she would not be responsible for more innocent lives.

Using the scope, she searched for zombies. After a second round of the barricades and the area within, she panned outward. It wasn't easy without proper lighting, and she glanced at her watch. It was a few minutes past four. Dawn would come soon, and she wished it would hurry.

A grating sound alerted her to company when the roof access door swung open. Timothy ducked through the opening, carrying a rifle. He smiled when he spotted her and walked over. "Hey, Sarah. Frank sent me to help you."

"That was kind of him," Sarah said.

"He asked us to check the streets below. They're going out to talk to the people next door and want to make sure it's safe before they go out," Mason said, waving a radio in one hand.

"That's easy enough," Sarah said, heading to the front of the building. She leaned over the edge and scanned the road below. It was empty, but she walked from end to end to make sure.

Timothy copied her before giving the area a general scan. "It looks clear."

"Pretty much. I haven't seen anything, zombie or otherwise," Sarah said.

"I'll tell Frank," Timothy said.

He relayed the news over the radio, and they watched as Frank and his group exited the station. They moved next door and talked to two women before inspecting the block. The entire time, Sarah and Timothy followed their progress through the scopes of their rifles.

"It seems kind of pointless," Timothy said. "There's nothing out there."

"Maybe, but Frank is a stickler for protocol. He believes in checking, double checking, and triple checking everything, no matter how trivial," Sarah said. "It's what made him so good at his job. He never missed anything."

"You admire him," Timothy said.

"I do," Sarah said. "He's my mentor, even if he doesn't realize it."

"What do you mean?"

"Oh, come on. You must've noticed that I can be annoyingly chirpy," Sarah said. "Especially to a crusty old dog like Frank. I irritate him."

"I don't know. I think you're cute," Timothy said.

Sarah choked back a laugh. "Cute? You think I'm cute? Puppies are cute."

"Er... sorry. I didn't mean it like that," Timothy said.

"I know. You just can't help it," Sarah said. "All people see when they look at me is a pretty girl with a big smile and a cheery attitude. They don't see the real me."

"Who is the real Sarah?" Timothy asked, his expression earnest.

"I am many things, Timothy. A person's personality is never a simple matter, but what I'm not is some delicate flower destined to work in a library and wear sundresses to the park," Sarah said. "I'm an officer of the law. I've dedicated my life to becoming strong so that I can protect the weak and punish evildoers, even if it is the zombie apocalypse."

"That's a lofty ideal and a worthy one," Timothy said.

"You make me sound conceited," Sarah said.

"Sorry; I didn't mean it like that," Timothy said, blushing bright red.

"I know. I'm just teasing," Sarah said with a grin. She leaned toward him. "So what makes Timothy tick?"

"I'm a simple guy," Timothy said. "I'm not complicated or deep. What you see is what you get."

"Somehow, I doubt that," Sarah said. "I think there's more to you than meets the eye."

"I want to help people. That's why I became a firefighter," Timothy added.

"And now it's the zombie apocalypse," Sarah said.

"I know. Who'd have thought?" Timothy said. He was quiet for a while before he continued. "I hope my family is okay. The last I heard, they were doing well, but that was days ago."

"I'm sure they're fine," Sarah said, laying a soft hand on his arm.

He smiled at her. "Thank you."

"Of course. We're all in this together," Sarah said. "The least we can do is be there for each other."

The radio at Timothy's side crackled, and he answered. "Yes, Sir?"

"We're coming back in, Timothy. The block is clear."

"Got it, Sir," Timothy said.

They watched as Frank's group returned to the fire station and waited until the bay doors closed behind them. Once they were safe inside, Sarah turned to Timothy. "Are you going back in?"

"I guess so," Timothy said with a shrug.

"I'll stay a little bit longer," Sarah said.

"Are you sure?"

"I'm sure."

"I can stay with you," Timothy offered.

"That's sweet, but I need a moment to gather my thoughts. It's been a long night," Sarah said.

"I understand, but don't take too long," Timothy said. "A hot cup of coffee will be waiting for you below."

"Thanks. I'll be right there," Sarah said. "Promise."

Timothy left her on the roof, going back to the others. Sarah walked toward the far end of the building and faced the northeast. There she waited, emptying her mind of all thought. She was a big believer in meditation and often used the method to calm herself in times of distress.

As the sun touched the far horizon, she lifted her face toward the sun. Its warmth touched her skin, and tendrils of its golden heat crept into her heart. Standing there, it was strangely peaceful, and she managed to forget her grief for a while. Maybe one day, it won't hurt so much anymore.

Finally, Sarah decided to go back. The night had gone, and morning had come. It was time to face whatever else life had to throw at them. Before she left, she raised her rifle and scanned the barricades one last time.

The area within the block remained empty of life, except for the occasional rat or feral cat scurrying through the alleyways. Panning the scope across the area beyond the barriers, she checked for activity.

With the coming dawn, she could make out a couple of figures roaming the streets. They wandered about aimlessly, and she guessed they were infected. It was good to know they hadn't been alerted by the previous night's activity. At least for now, their haven remained undetected. Hidden.

Her stomach growled, and she determined it was time for breakfast. It was bound to be a long day, and she'd need her strength, especially since she was operating on the minimum amount of sleep.

As she prepared to leave, Sarah caught a glimpse of something different. A vehicle driving slowly along the row. As it neared the barricade, it stopped, idling in one spot. Then it reversed, going back the way it came.

As it turned a corner, Sarah caught a glimpse of bright red. She waited for a few more minutes, but it never returned. Finally, she straightened up and walked to the roof access. There was no point wasting any more time, and she needed to tell Frank what she'd seen. *And I can grab a cup of coffee at the same time—two birds with one stone.*

Chapter 13 - Francis

An infected woman stumbled down the street, dragging a broken leg. Every time she stepped on the limb, the bones ground together, further mangling the flesh. She didn't notice or care. Nor did she feel a thing. The only sensation she felt was the gnawing pit of hunger in her stomach. It drove her ever onward in search of food, and she wandered tirelessly until she found it.

A name tag on the woman's chest read Francis. That was who she used to be in her former life. A young woman working her way through college and earning money as a waitress at a local coffee shop. Attractive and neat, she had a practiced smile and easygoing manner, all traits that earned her good tips, especially from the regulars.

Francis was smart enough to learn their names, favorite meals, and just enough about their daily lives and family to make it seem personal. To make them think she cared. It wasn't hard. People liked to talk about themselves.

Things went well until Mrs. Jenkins entered the coffee shop, acting funny. Her arm was heavily bandaged, and she seemed off balance and confused. Heat radiated from her skin, and she fell into the nearest booth as if her legs couldn't hold her anymore. There she sat, nursing a cup of coffee until she dozed off.

"Mrs. Jenkins, are you feeling okay?" Francis had asked, touching the woman's shoulder.

Mrs. Jenkins jerked around and snarled at Francis, her eyes bloodshot and crazed. Saliva frothed on her lips, and Francis stumbled back in horror.

"Mrs. Jenkins? What are you—"

Mrs. Jenkins snapped at the air, baring her teeth like a rabid dog. She cocked her head and eyed Francis with evil intent. Shrieking like a banshee, she attacked.

"Mrs. Jenkins, what are you—" Francis screamed, turning to run. Before she'd gone three steps, clawed hands dug into her shoulder, and she spun around. Her ankle twisted, and she went down with Mrs. Jenkins on top of her.

Her leg snapped like a twig, and white-hot pain lanced up her leg. She screamed, but her voice was cut off when sharp teeth tore into her throat. Blood fountained from the wound, and she stared at the crimson spray with a sense of disbelief. *No, this can't be happening.*

Twisting away from the snapping teeth, Francis crawled across the floor. Her broken leg dragged behind her, the sharp end of the tibia sticking out through the flesh. Blood pumped from the hole in her throat, warm and sticky. The essence of life.

Screams of fear rose around her as the other customers panicked. The noise drew Mrs. Jenkins away from her victim, and she launched herself at an older man in a wheelchair. She ripped into his face, tearing through the papery skin like it was nothing, and people scattered in all directions. Chairs fell over, and cutlery smashed to pieces as chaos broke out in the shop.

Francis crawled across the floor, but her strength was waning. She searched for help and spotted a slender man in a business suit. Reaching out with a trembling hand, she pleaded. "Help me, please!"

The stranger stared at her with horrified fascination, his spectacles perched on the end of his nose. His lips quivered with fright, and he shook his head. "I'm sorry. I can't."

On unsteady legs, he ran away, and Francis' last hope died. Sagging to the cold tiles, she choked back a sob. "Someone, please. Help me."

Lying in a pool of her own blood, she felt the life drain from her body. Her vision dimmed, and the light faded from her eyes. Breathing her last, Francis was gone, along with her hopes, dreams, and ambitions.

In her place rose a monster, and like all monsters, she needed to feed. What she craved was flesh. Warm, living flesh. Breakfast consisted of a rat unlucky enough to get too close, and the day before, she'd feasted on the flesh of a teen boy. He'd left his hiding spot and gone on a supply run. Inside the shop, he'd dropped a can of beans, alerting the zombies outside to his presence. That mistake proved to be his last.

Now she was on the hunt again, prowling the avenues of her former home in search of prey. Movement drew her attention, as did sound and smell. When an ambulance cruised past her in the street, she gave chase. When it stopped, she closed in, beating her fists on its bright red sides.

But she soon tired of the game. Nothing living could be seen through the tinted windows, and the metal contraption stank of smoke and burning fuel. It smelled not of flesh and blood, and she saw nothing that indicated food.

Losing interest, Francis continued on her way. A block

further, she met up with two more of her kind. They didn't mean anything to her, and she felt no kinship, but they were going the same way. She fell in beside them, and they formed a small group. More of the undead joined them along the way, and their numbers grew apace. That continued until they reached a corner.

Above their heads loomed a multi-storied building, the Virtua Willingboro Hospital. A fence surrounded the property, reinforced with barbed wire, concrete slabs, and metal sheets. The gates were likewise closed, sealed off by double-layered barricades.

It was impossible to see inside the grounds, all views blocked by the mish-mash of material that lined the palisades. It effectively hid its contents from prying eyes but couldn't block out the sound of voices from within.

The zombies, numbering over a hundred strong, paused a few feet from the nearest gate. As one, they turned toward the noise, and their appetites quickened with the promise of fresh meat.

The undead mob charged the barricade, their feet thundering across the asphalt. Their lips peeled back from their teeth, and they snarled with primitive rage. Closing on their objective, they failed to notice the barrel of a fifty-caliber machine gun mounted on a turret. Even if they had, they wouldn't have known what it was or cared.

Francis ran with the rest, her predatory instinct urging her onward. She raced toward the gate, determined to get to the prey that hid behind its reinforced steel. Her stomach clamored with anticipation, and the virus in her brain urged her to feed.

Suddenly, the fifty caliber's muzzle flashed. A wall of red-hot lead cut through the mob, ripping their bodies to shreds. Heads exploded, limbs flew, and torsos burst. Brains, guts, bodily fluids, and innards paved the road, and the tar grew slick with blood.

Francis never saw the bullet that ended her undead life. It flew across the distance, faster than the speed of sound, and punched into her forehead. It traveled through her brain and blasted out the back of her skull. Thrown backward, she landed on her back, her broken leg bent at an obscene angle.

When the last zombie fell, the fifty caliber's muzzle stopped turning, and silence fell across the bloody scene. A few minutes passed before the gate opened with a ponderous groan. Six armed figures exited the gate and fanned out. With their guns at the ready, they moved through the ranks of the fallen undead.

A snarl sounded when an infected reared its head. A bullet from the fifty-caliber gun had cut it in half, but it was still alive. A muffled pop sounded, and one of the figures dispatched the zombie for good.

That continued until the team of armed guards checked the entire area, focusing entirely on their surroundings. Afterward, they returned to the gate and gathered inside the entrance to discuss the situation.

"We'd better get the clean-up crew out here," the first voice said.

"Yup, the fifty sure makes a mess, Lieutenant," a second voice replied.

"More will come," the lieutenant agreed. "The noise draws them like moths to a flame."

"We could send out an ambo, Lieutenant."

"Ambo 27 just got back an hour ago, Chris," the lieutenant

replied.

"What about Ambo 33?" Chris suggested. "Banks won't mind. He hates being cooped up in the hospital. Zoey too."

"Those two are crazy," a feminine voice said. "Riding around day and night in a city overrun with those things? Crazy, I tell you."

"Yeah, they're nuts, Priya," Chris said, "but they bring back valuable intel. Besides, the infected don't seem to bother them."

"Yeah, I suppose as long as they can't see or hear you, they don't give chase," Priya agreed.

"I'll find Banks and ask him to draw off the infected," the lieutenant commanded. "Chris, you get the clean-up crew ready."

"Yes, Sir," Chris replied.

"The rest of you, make sure nothing gets in. Living or dead. Priya's in charge," the lieutenant added.

"Yes, Sir," a chorus of voices replied.

The gate closed with a clang, and everyone took up their positions. Out in the street, not a soul stirred, the area devoid of life. A chill breeze swept through the trees, and a flock of ravens flew overhead. Then the first infected showed, drawn by the noise from before. Another reared its head, and another, and another. Soon, they came from all directions, zeroing in on the hospital.

Before they could swarm the area, the gate opened, and an ambulance drove through the entrance. It drove through the throng and switched on its sirens. With the lights flashing, it drew the undead away from the hospital.

While the zombies knew what was food and what wasn't, the blaring noise, coupled with the lights, proved too tempting to ignore. As one, they followed the vehicle, running as fast as their bodies allowed. Within minutes, peace was restored, and Priya chuckled. "Just another day in the apocalypse."

Chapter 14 - Zoey

The ambulance cruised down the street, a silent witness to a broken world. Inside its protective shell sat two people. Banks operated the wheel while Zoey lounged in the passenger seat next to him. Outside, it was still dark, though dawn wasn't far off, and the weather was typical for late fall: Cold and miserable.

Zoey shivered when a chill ran down her spine and burrowed deeper into her jacket's collar. She stared out the window, taking in the bleak scenery. Already, Burlington looked like something out of an apocalyptic movie. The streets were empty except for the abandoned cars, rotting corpses, and strewn rubbish.

Weeds poked up through the pavement cracks, and the recent rains had eroded the street, forming giant potholes. Infected wandered the streets, their eyes soulless, their bodies mere vessels for the virus inside their brains.

They appeared to be in a fugue state, almost as if they were in a trance. Not even the moving ambulance was enough to jar them awake. Only the sight of warm flesh shocked them back to the land of the living. Food.

It was what they lived for. It was what the virus wanted. Not only did feeding on the living nourish their bodies, but it spread the infection. More hosts for the virus within their brains.

Weaving around the road hazards, Zoey smothered a laugh when she spotted a zombie stuck inside a pothole. The trench was waist-deep, and the dumb creature snarled with futile rage when a rat scurried past. The rodent paused mid-scurry to test the air, its nose twitching. It stayed just beyond the zombie's reach, smart enough not to get caught. Finally, it lost interest and moved on, disappearing into a dark alleyway. *Smart mouse.*

"Are you hungry?" Banks asked, pulling her from her reverie.

"I could eat," Zoey said with a shrug.

"Wait here," Banks said, pulling to a stop.

He removed a metal pipe from underneath his seat, one end sharpened to a fine point. After a quick check to ensure the coast was clear, he jumped up and ran into a convenience store. It wasn't long before he returned. They'd hit the store many times before and knew it was zombie free.

Banks returned moments later and climbed back into the ambo. Rummaging through a plastic bag, he tossed a couple of items into her lap. "I got your favorite."

Zoey picked up the bag of Flamin' Hot Cheetos and a packet of Reese's Peanut Butter Cups and grinned. "Aw, aren't you a sweetheart?"

"You know what they say: Breakfast is the most important meal of the day," Banks replied.

"I don't think this junk counts as real food," Zoey said.

"It does now," Banks said, digging into a jar of Jiffy peanut butter.

Silence fell over the cab while they ate, broken only by the crunch of crackers, chips, and foil packets. Afterward, they cracked a couple of ice-cold cokes and cheered each other.

"Here's to you and me. Paramedics by day, recon specialists, and zombie bait by night," Zoey said.

"Hear, hear," Banks replied.

Zoey drained her coke in one big gulp, savoring the fizz in her throat. Crumpling up the can, she tossed it into their trash bag and let rip a giant burp. "Ah, that's better."

"Could you not do that?" Banks exclaimed, wrinkling his nose. "We've talked about this."

"It's just a little bit of gas. Now, if it came out the other end, that would be a real problem," she replied with a chuckle.

"Please, don't. I'm begging you," Banks said, rolling his eyes.

"So, what's the plan? We've been out all night. We led the zombies away from the hospital and scoured the area. Time to head back?"

"Maybe, but I want to check something out first," Banks said.

"That roadblock we spotted earlier?" Zoey asked.

"Yes, it was too dark to see properly before, and I didn't want to use the lights," Banks explained.

"I know, but it'll be dawn soon," Zoey said. "We can take a second look."

"Exactly," Banks said. "Lieutenant Kingsley would want us to check it out."

"Well, what are you waiting for?" Zoey said, waving him on. "We don't have all day."

"Yes, we do. We literally have all day," Banks said. "That's all we do now. Cruise the streets looking for survivors, places to raid, that sort of thing."

"I know, but I'm ready for a hot shower and a proper breakfast. Driving around with you is fun and all, but I miss my bed," Zoey said.

"Do you miss your bed, or what's waiting for you inside it?"

Banks asked with a grin.

Zoey's cheeks reddened. "That's none of your business."

"Oh, come on. You know I live vicariously through you. You're my only outlet," Banks said.

"My relationship is none of your business," Zoey said, throwing him a warning look.

"But I'm single and lonely," Banks protested.

"It's not my fault no woman wants to hook up with that ugly face," Zoey said with a cheeky grin.

"Wow, that hurt," Banks said with an expression of mock hurt. "Who wouldn't want a stud like me?"

"Not me," Zoey said, rolling her eyes.

"That's because I'm not your type."

"You've got that right," Zoey said. "Men aren't my type."

"Can't say I blame you."

"Seriously, though. You're a great guy, Banks. You could get a girl if you let her close. The problem is, you won't let anyone see the real you. Nobody but me."

"Whatever," Banks grumbled, deflecting like he always did.

Zoey inwardly shook her head. When they were alone, Banks was a different person. Warm, funny, and approachable. But he changed when they were among other people, becoming cold and distant. It was a defense mechanism, and she understood why he did it. As long as he didn't get close to anyone, he couldn't get hurt. She was the only one he allowed near him, probably because they'd been working together for years. *Poor Banks. I hope he lets down his walls one day and lets someone in. Someone other than me.*

When they reached the barricade, it was still dark, and Banks parked the ambulance. "We might as well get comfy. Dawn is still a half hour away."

"Then I'm catching a nap. See ya," Zoey said.

She lifted her feet onto the dashboard and shifted in her seat, trying to get comfortable. The ambulance's cab wasn't exactly cozy, even for someone of her short stature. She folded her arms and leaned her head against the headrest. Closing her eyes, she dozed off. Sleep. Blessed, wonderful sleep.

"Zoey, wake up!" Banks barked.

"Huh? What?" Zoey mumbled, jerking upright. She bumped her head against the window frame, and she winced. "Ow."

"It's time," Banks said.

"Okay, but you didn't have to give me such a fright," Zoey said.

"Why not? It's fun," Banks said with a wink.

He started the engine and cruised up to the barricade. Rolling to a stop, they investigated the structure before he reversed and drove back to the hospital. "It's definitely man-made."

"Yup," Zoey agreed. "The question is, are they friendly or not?"

"I guess we'll find out soon enough," Banks said.

Parking the ambo in a deserted alleyway, Banks raised the hospital on his radio. He managed to contact Lieutenant Kingsley, who listened with interest to his report.

"Stick around, Banks. I'll see if we can contact them on the radio. If they sound legit, we'll set up a meeting. Over," Lieutenant Kingsley said.

"Sure thing, Lieutenant," Banks agreed. "Out."

"Guess we're stuck out here for a bit longer," Banks said.

"Ah, well. At least it's peaceful," Zoey said, chewing on one thumbnail. "I wonder who these people are."

"Me too."

"We could use more hands. People are becoming scarce. Good people, that is," Banks said.

"Too true," Zoey said with a sigh. "Besides, your future girlfriend could be out there somewhere."

"Shut it, Zoey," Banks said with a warning growl.

She laughed, not at all intimidated by his gruff nature. "You know you love me."

"Yes, you're the little sister I always hoped I'd never have," he replied.

She opened her mouth to reply, loving the banter but was interrupted.

The radio crackled, and Banks answered. "Banks, here. Over."

"We contacted the survivors. They're firefighters occupying the firehouse and the block around it. Over," Lieutenant Kingsley said.

"For real? Firefighters? Over." Banks asked.

"They sound legit," Kingsley said. "I want you to meet with them in two hours at the barricade. Over."

"Just us?" Banks asked with a doubtful frown. "Over."

"I could send someone to assist, but I think these guys are on the level," Kingsley explained. "Even so, be careful. Over."

"Copy that. Out," Banks said.

Zoey leaned back in her seat and groaned. "Two more hours?"

"Yup."

"I'm going to need more snacks."

"I thought you might," Banks said, rummaging around beneath his seat. He produced another packet of Flamin' Hot Cheetos with a flourish. "Ta-da!"

"Banks, I take back every mean thing I've ever said to you,"

Zoey cried, grabbing the packet. "You are the best."

"Of course I am," Banks said with a smug look.

Settling back into her seat, Zoey dug into the chips with glee. "Now we wait."

Chapter 15 - Susan

Susan set out the plates, cutlery, and napkins before standing back to survey her handiwork. The food was ready and sat in the middle of the table, along with a selection of condiments. They'd managed to whip up a stack of pancakes with butter, syrup, and canned strawberries. There was also a big bowl of scrambled eggs with veggies, or mishmash eggs, as Ellen called it.

"Here we go," Ellen said, adding two jugs of reconstituted orange juice and two more jugs filled with water.

"The coffee is ready, I made tea, and I washed all the dishes," Amelia said, wiping her hands with a dishcloth.

"Excellent. Thank you so much, guys," Susan said. "Let's take a break before the first lot arrive."

"Sounds like a plan," Ellen said, pouring each of them a cup of coffee. They sat down around the table and fell into a companionable silence. The stresses of the night before melted away as the hot brew warmed their stomachs, and Susan heaved a sigh of relief. "I'm glad it's over."

"Me too," Ellen said. "But we paid a heavy price last night."

"Yes, we did," Amelia said, her expression sad. "It will take a while before we recover as a group."

"Yes, but I also think things could have gone a lot worse, and it still might in the days to come," Susan said. "We're still at the beginning of the apocalypse."

"Yes, if you look at the math, the odds are not in our favor," Amelia said. "Once this infection hits maximum saturation, there will be millions, even billions of them, and just a few of us."

"That's comforting," Ellen said in a wry voice.

"Amelia has always been good with numbers," Susan said. "At least we have one thing the zombies don't have. Brains."

"It's always been that way for humanity. We started with nothing but our intelligence and became the apex predator on the planet," Amelia mused. "Now the zombies are the apex predators."

"Not if we can help it, right?" Susan asked.

"Right," Amelia said with a determined nod.

"What did I miss?" Ruby asked, entering the kitchen.

"Breakfast is ready if you're hungry," Susan said.

"I'm starving," Ruby said.

"How's George doing?" Amelia asked.

"He's sleeping. I gave him as much pain medication as I dared, and he's off in dreamland," Ruby said. "Other than that, he's stable."

"I'll pray for a quick recovery," Ellen said.

"I just hope we got the arm off in time," Ruby said. "If the infection managed to spread…."

"Shouldn't he be in quarantine?" Ellen asked. "What if he attacks Theresa?"

"Theresa is ready for it," Ruby said. "She'll manage."

"George will be fine," Susan said with as much confidence as she could muster. Despair never did any good; she'd had enough of the glum expressions. "Coffee or tea, Ruby?"

"Tea, please," Ruby said, taking a seat.

Susan poured her a cup and waved at the food. "We might as well eat. The rest will show up when they're done doing whatever they're doing."

"Don't mind if I do," Ellen said, grabbing a plate. She piled it high with food and crammed a mouthful of pancakes and syrup into her mouth.

Susan watched her with a smile of private amusement, wondering where it all went. As thin as a rake, Ellen never failed to amaze Susan with her prodigious appetite. *That girl eats like a horse yet never picks up a single milligram. It's so unfair.*

Spooning up a small amount of scrambled eggs, two pancakes, and a pat of butter and strawberries, Susan sat down to eat her meal. Unlike Ellen, she had to watch every bite that passed her lips or risk packing on the pounds, a big no-no for a firefighter. She also spent a lot of time in the gym, determined to stay fit and strong. It was for her own good.

While she ate, her thoughts wandered to Noah, and she wondered how he was doing. Not a moment passed that she didn't worry about her son, and it killed her that she couldn't talk to him. The cellphone lines never reopened after the first crash, and the Internet was extremely spotty. The last time she got an email from him was three days ago, and it scared her silly to think of him wandering around in a hostile zombie-filled world. But what could she do besides suffer in silence? Everybody had their own cross to bear. She was nothing special.

While she ate, the rest of the station began to trickle into the kitchen, and the clatter of plates and cutlery filled the air. Frank's team was the first, fresh from their inspection of the block, followed shortly by Robert and his team. Timothy showed up minutes later, leaving only Bobbi, Sarah, and Theresa out of the loop.

Once she'd finished her food, Susan dished a plate and poured a cup of tea. "I'm taking this to Theresa, guys. Enjoy your food, but I expect this place to be spotless when I get back. Ellen and Amelia are excused from cleaning duties."

"Yes, ma'am," the rest mumbled through mouths full of food. "Good."

Entering Theresa's office, she found the woman sitting in a chair next to an unconscious George's bed. "I brought you something to eat, Theresa."

"Thank you," Theresa said, putting her book down. "I appreciate that."

"How's our patient?"

"Resting, I hope. He needs it," Theresa said, taking a sip of tea.

"That he does," Susan said. "Are you sure you should be alone with him?"

"I'll be fine. I think we got it in time," Theresa said.

"I can stay with you," Susan offered.

"No, thank you. It's bad enough that one of us is stuck here, let alone two," Theresa said. "You must have a lot to do."

"Alright, I'm going, but I'll be back for your dishes," Susan said, returning to the kitchen. Taking another plate, she dished up for Bobbi and prepared to take it to her. Before she could move, however, clattering footsteps announced a ruddy-cheeked Sarah, fresh from the roof.

Sarah headed straight for the coffee pot. "Boy, could I use a shot of caffeine right about now." She poured herself a cup, spooned in roughly a pound of sugar, added a touch of milk, and turned to survey the room. "So? What have I missed?"

"Well, you almost missed breakfast," Susan said, her tone wry.

"Not for long," Sarah said. "But before I eat, I saw something beyond the barricade."

"What did you see?" Robert asked, perking up.

"A vehicle. A red one. It was hard to determine exactly what it was, but I saw it," Sarah said.

"Did it come close?" Robert asked.

"It approached the barricade, stopped for a while, then left," Sarah said.

"I wonder who they were and what they wanted," Robert mused.

"I don't know, but I think we should permanently post a guard on the roof," Sarah suggested.

"I agree," Frank said.

"I'll go back up as soon as I've eaten," Sarah offered.

"Thank you," Robert said. "We'll send someone to take over from you in a while."

"Deal," Sarah said, refilling her cup.

"Did I hear something about a strange vehicle?" Bobbi said, showing up.

"You heard right," Sarah said with a nod.

"Well, I just spoke to them on the radio. They say hi," Bobbi said.

"What?" Frank said, jerking around in his seat.

"You heard me," Bobbi said.

"Who are they?" Robert asked.

"They're paramedics from Virtua Willingboro Hospital. Apparently, there's a whole group of survivors living there."

"What do they want?" Robert asked.

"They want to meet with us," Bobbi said.

Robert and Frank exchanged looks.

"What do I tell them?" Bobbi asked.

"Tell them we'll let them know," Robert said. "Once we've had time to sort things out. I'll clear it with Theresa."

"Okay, I'll do that," Bobbi said, inclining her head.

"Take something to eat," Susan said, handing her a plate of food and a cup of coffee.

"Thanks," Bobbi said, taking her leave.

"We should have a meeting to discuss last night's events and this new development," Frank said.

"Yes, we should," Robert agreed.

"What about Donna, Sam, and Andrea?" Susan asked.

"They deserve a proper burial," Amelia said.

"As much as that's true, it's not possible," Robert said. "We have to burn the bodies."

"We can at least have a short ceremony," Amelia protested. "Pay our respects."

"Alright. We can do that after breakfast," Robert said. "Then we'll take them to the lot for cremation."

"I'll go with you," Frank said.

"Me too," Leo said. "Donna was our friend."

"Sounds good. I'll need the help, and afterward, we can meet the newcomers at the barricade," Robert said. "Find out what they want."

"What about the meeting?" Susan asked.

"We can have it after that, and everyone should be there," Robert said. "Including Bobbi and Theresa."

"I'll let them know," Susan said, "and I'll make sure there's coffee."

"Thank you, Susan; I can always count on you. We all can," Robert said.

"I'm standing guard. Someone has to keep an eye out for danger with all these strange folks around," Sarah said.

"She's right. We should be careful," Frank cautioned.

"Fair enough. We'll make sure we're armed and ready when we meet them. We'll take a radio too," Robert said. "The rest of you must be prepared to defend this place if necessary."

"We'll be ready," Mason said.

"You can count on us," Clare added.

"What about the people next door? They'll want to attend the meeting," Mason said.

"You should inform them of the time then," Robert said.

"No problem. I'll pop around after the service," Mason said.

"I'll go with you," Clare said. "I'd like to say hello to Paisley."

"Yeah, right," Mason scoffed. "You just want to tag along and ruin my day."

"Busted," Clare replied with a grin.

"Whatever," Robert said. "Just get it done."

"Will do," Clare said, unrepentant.

"Okay. Are we done now?" Mason said. "All this talking is interfering with my breakfast."

Robert sighed. "Yes, we are done."

"Thanks," Mason said, shoveling a forkful of pancakes into his mouth. He washed it down with a glass of orange juice, groaning with satisfaction. "Now that's what I'm talking about."

"Glad you're enjoying my pancakes," Amelia said with an amused look.

"Oh, I am," Mason said.

"In that case, you can wash the dishes. Consider it a thank you," Amelia said.

Clare laughed out loud with glee. "Sucker!"

But she sobered when Amelia added. "Just for that, you can help him, Clare."

"Clare's face fell, and it was Mason's turn to laugh.

Susan watched the scene with a sense of contentment. Despite everything that had happened, it was good to see people laughing. It was even better to know they still had the capacity. It meant they still had hope, and that was a powerful thing.

Chapter 16 - Robert

After breakfast, everyone moved to the garage. Robert, Leo, and Frank loaded the bodies of Donna, Sam, and Andrea onto stretchers. These they placed in the back of the nearest fire truck before turning to face the gathered crowd.

"Would anyone like to say a few words?" Robert asked.

"I do," Frank said, raising a hand. He cleared his throat and looked around. "I did not know Donna that well. She worked with me, but we weren't friends. Even so, she was never anything but kind to me and everyone she interacted with. She loved her job, and she worked hard—both for herself and others. I'm sorry that I couldn't save her, and I'm even sorrier that her illness caused the deaths of others. I'll always feel guilty for that, and I will try my best to make it up to this community."

"It wasn't your fault, Frank. We all missed it," Robert said, placing one hand on the man's shoulder.

"Thank you, but I was responsible for her," Frank said, his expression bleak.

Robert shook his head, saddened. "Anyone else?"

Bobbi stepped forward. "Like the rest of you, I didn't know Andrea. We hardly spoke, and we didn't have much in common, but she loved animals, which I can relate to." Nods of agreement did the rounds, and Bobbi continued. "And I promise I'll take care of Sebastian to the best of my ability."

She stepped back, and Amelia raised her hand. "I'd like to say something about Sam. We spent a day and a night trapped together inside my old office. He was kind and funny. He was just a kid who tried to cope as best he could in a terrible situation. I will miss him, as I'm sure we all will."

"May they rest in peace," Robert added. "Let's have a moment of silence."

A deep hush fell across the gathering, each saying goodbye in their way. For Robert, it was a pivotal moment. They'd lost something that night—their sense of invulnerability. The station was no longer the fortress it'd been before. The safe haven that protected them from the world outside. The monsters had gotten in, killing them from the inside out, and nothing would be the same again. *Will any of us be able to trust in our safety again? Will we have to sleep with one eye open for the rest of our lives?*

The likely answer to those questions was yes, and that knowledge weighed heavy on him. He felt the burden of responsibility more than ever, and he wondered if he was up to the task.

After a minute had passed, Robert broke the silence. "Thank you for coming, guys. Frank, Leo, and I will take the bodies for cremation. After that, we're meeting with the newcomers at the barricade. Hopefully, it won't take long, and we'll be back in time for the meeting."

"Are you letting the strangers in?" Mike asked.

"No, we're meeting with them, that's all. Nothing more," Robert said.

"Alright. We'll be ready for trouble, though," Mike added.

"Just in case."

Robert nodded. "We'll stay in touch via radio."

"Be careful," Theresa said.

"We will," Robert said.

Theresa left, making her way back to George's side. The rest of the group dispersed to do their own thing. Mason, Clare, Mike, Elijah, Timothy, and Benjamin were the only exceptions. They stayed behind to stand guard in case of trouble while Sarah returned to the roof with her rifle.

With the service behind them, Robert, Leo, and Frank climbed into the truck. They were each armed with a handgun and an ax, while Frank carried a shotgun for good measure. They exited the station and drove toward an empty concrete lot with a small park in the middle.

It was the only open space near them, and they'd begun using it to cremate the infected. Afterward, the remains were placed in a shallow grave and covered with a thin layer of dirt. It was the first time they were burning human corpses, and they completed the task with heavy hearts.

Robert watched the flames race along the path they'd created with the accelerant, a squirt of gasoline. The cover sheets charred, split apart, and peeled back to reveal the bodies underneath. He backed away when the sickly sweet stench of burning flesh hit his nostrils. It was a horrendous smell, and he didn't want to risk losing his breakfast.

Leo and Frank followed, watching from a distance as the flames consumed their former friends. When the fire died, they buried the remains in a shallow grave and scattered a layer of dirt over the top.

With the burial behind them, Robert looked around. The park, though small, was pretty. A couple of tall trees cast dappled shadows on the ground, and birds chattered in the trees. Flowers bloomed in the corners, adding a cheerful touch, and clouds drifted across the blue sky overhead. "This isn't so bad, I guess."

"No, it's not," Leo agreed.

"I'll say a prayer, and we can go," Frank said.

Eternal rest grant unto them, O Lord. And let perpetual light shine upon them. May they rest in peace. Amen.

It was short and simple, but the words were final, and Robert felt better when they left. As they climbed into the truck, he drove away with a sense of completion. One chapter of his life was over, and he was about to enter another—a survivor's life.

When they reached the barrier, the ambulance was already waiting. It sat on the other side, a silent sentinel. Coming to a stop, Robert surveyed the area. It appeared to be quiet, and he reached for his radio. "Sarah. Sarah, come in. Over."

"This is Sarah. Over."

"What does it look like?" Robert asked. "Over."

"I've looked everywhere. It's clean. Over."

"Can we proceed? Over."

"Yes, but be careful. I don't know what's inside the ambulance. Over," Sarah said.

"Copy that. Out," Robert said. He patted the gun at his side. "I guess this is it."

"I'll cover you from here," Frank offered, brandishing his shotgun.

"Thanks," Robert said.

"I'll go with you," Leo said.

Together, they exited the vehicle and walked toward the barricade. The doors to the ambulance opened, and two people climbed out. The first figure was a tall man with charcoal skin, cropped hair, and golden-brown eyes. The second was a woman with red hair and creamy white skin. The kind that blistered after five minutes in the sun.

They faced each other across the distance, and the man spoke first. "Thank you for agreeing to meet us. My name is Banks, and this is Zoey."

"Nice to meet you," Zoey said with a slight wave, her red hair shining in the sunlight.

Robert nodded. "I got your message, and I am glad you reached out to us. I'm Robert, this is Leo, and that's Frank."

"Are you with the fire station?" Banks asked, pointing at the fire truck.

"I am a firefighter, yes, but Frank and Leo are police officers," Robert answered.

At his words, Zoey perked up. "The police? We thought you were all gone. The City department was overrun, and we couldn't find any survivors. It's the same with the Township department."

"We're from the City department, and as far as we know, only the three of us are left," Leo said.

"Only three?" Zoey said with a gasp. "I'm so sorry."

"Thanks," Leo said.

"What about you?" Robert asked.

"We are paramedics with the Virtua Willingboro hospital," Banks said.

"I'm surprised the hospital survived. That's like ground zero, isn't it?" Leo asked. "You must've been flooded with infected."

"We were. People flocked to us in the hundreds, and everyone who died returned to life. We would've been overrun if it wasn't for SCERT," Banks said.

"SCERT?" Leo said. "The Sheriff's Emergency Response

Team?"

"That's the one," Banks said. "They eliminated the zombies, quarantined the infected, and cleared the ground level and trauma unit. After that, they closed the parking area, blocked the gates, and set up a perimeter."

"So, the hospital is zombie free?" Robert asked.

"Not exactly. The morgue is full of them. The upper levels too. We survivors stick to the ground floor and the trauma unit," Banks explained.

"Isn't that dangerous?" Robert asked.

"The upper levels are blocked off. They can't get out," Banks explained.

"How many of you are there?" Robert said.

"A few dozen. Mostly doctors, nurses, hospital staff, and former patients. We've had civilians trickle in over time, but not many people are left out there. It's mostly zombies now."

"That's why we were so excited when we found you. I knew this barricade was made on purpose, and we heard a gunshot during the night," Zoey said with an enthusiastic grin.

"We had some problems. An outbreak inside the station," Robert admitted with a pained look. "We lost three people."

"I'm sorry to hear that," Banks said. "Did you manage to contain it?"

"Yes, we did, and we'll be more careful in the future," Robert said.

"We've learned the hard way, too," Banks said. "This apocalypse… it's something else. That's another reason we wanted to meet."

"Yes?" Robert asked.

"We want to form an alliance and work together," Banks said. "It's the only way we'll survive in the long run. Not all survivors are friendly."

"Have you had problems?" Robert asked.

"Not yet, but some of the people we've taken in have been robbed or worse. The zombies aren't our only enemies. There are other people, not to mention the threat of starvation and disease," Banks said.

"An alliance, you say? What would that entail exactly?" Robert said.

"That depends on you. We were thinking about opening trade between us and offering protection to one another," Banks said. "Of course, you need not decide anything now. We've merely come to touch base and to show you we're friendly."

"Trade and protection. A powerful duo," Robert mused.

"We can offer medicine and medical expertise, and we have the SCERT. Do you have any wounded that need treatment, perhaps?" Banks said.

Robert and Leo exchanged looks.

"One of our men had an amputation this morning. He was bitten, so we removed the arm," Robert said.

"I imagine it was a traumatic experience without the proper medical facilities?" Banks said.

"We did well enough. We have trained and experienced EMTs on our side," Robert said.

"Maybe, but no anesthetic," Banks said. "And what if he develops an infection?"

"We'll cross that bridge when we get to it," Robert said.

"I understand, but please consider our offer of friendship. We'll be stronger if we stand together," Banks said.

"I'll relay the message," Robert said. "We'll be in touch via radio."

"I look forward to hearing from you," Banks said, inclining his head.

"Don't wait too long," Zoey said with a broad smile. "I'm dying to meet new people."

"Zoey, please. Contain yourself," Banks said, climbing back into their ambulance.

"What? I'm just being friendly. Besides, it's true," Zoey said, joining him on the passenger side. Before she closed the door, she waved. "Bye!"

Robert and Leo watched them drive away with a sense of bemusement.

"That was interesting," Leo said. "Trade and protection. It's not a bad deal."

"No, it's not," Robert said.

They turned and walked back to the truck where Franks waited, ready to blast a hole in anything that moved. "How did it go?"

"Quite well. We'll fill you in on the way back," Robert said.

"One thing, though," Leo said.

"What?" Frank asked.

"I think we just met Sarah's clone."

"Sarah's clone?" Frank repeated with a confused look.

"Or her long-lost twin," Robert said.

"Really?" Franks said.

Robert looked at Leo, and they both nodded.

"I'm going with twin. Non-identical in looks, though they both have red hair," Robert said.

"Yeah, but Sarah's hair is more of a reddish-gold," Leo mused. "Zoey's is darker."

"Really?" Frank said. "You're going on about hair color?"

"It was just an observation," Leo said, a blush rising up his cheeks, much to Robert's amusement.

He chuckled. "Whatever their differences in looks, they're almost identical in personality."

"You nailed it," Leo agreed, climbing into the truck.

As Robert slid behind the wheel, he mused about the vagaries of fate. Who'd have thought they'd meet possible new friends from a possibly friendly community? *This day can't get any weirder.*

Chapter 17 - Theresa

Theresa checked on George one last time before she left the room. It was time for the meeting, and she had to attend. After checking his heart rate and blood pressure, she checked his IV bag and patted his hand. "I'll be back soon, dear. Don't worry."

He couldn't hear her, of course. He was heavily sedated and fast asleep, but it felt right. Although he appeared to be doing well, she worried about him. She worried about all of her flock, but the young ones always tugged at her heartstrings.

After a final look, she left the room and locked the door, just in case. With her .38 Rossi tucked into its holster on her belt, she made her way to the kitchen.

Susan met her with a warm smile and a fresh cup of tea. "How are you holding up?"

"I'm alright, just tired," Theresa said.

"I'll watch over George for a spell after the meeting," Susan offered.

"Thank you. I could use a hot shower," Theresa said, and she wasn't lying.

Looking around the room, she determined that everyone was present except one. "Where's Sarah?"

"She's standing guard on the roof," Robert explained. "I thought it would be prudent now that other forces are on the board."

"Good thinking," Theresa said with an approving nod. She also noticed three extra people: Two women and a man. She recognized them as part of the teacher and parent group next door. Walking toward them, she said, "Welcome. I'm Theresa."

"I'm Sandi," one of the women replied. "We've met before. I'm a teacher."

"I remember, yes," Theresa said.

"And this is Claudia. She sought refuge at the school when the rising began," Sandi said.

The other woman sniffed. "I wouldn't call it a refuge. More like bad luck."

Ignoring her, Sandi continued. "This is James, a parent. He's been a great help to us, and I thought he should come along today."

"Of course," Theresa said, shaking his hand. "We are happy to have you."

"Thank you, ma'am. Happy to be here," James said.

Taking her seat at the head of the table, Theresa waited until everyone had settled down before she cleared her throat. "Good morning, everyone. Let's get this meeting started."

The hum of quiet conversation died down, and silence fell across the room. Nodding with approval, she continued. "I'll start with a brief recounting of last night's events. That should get all of us on the same page."

"Yes, please. I would love to know exactly what happened," Claudia said, her manner stiff. Unlike the night before, she was dressed in a pantsuit, and her hair was drawn back into a tight knot. This gave her a severe look that matched the bitter downturn of her lips.

Theresa noticed the petulant note in Claudia's voice and

immediately pegged her as a troublemaker. *We'll have to watch this one.*

Forcing a smile, she said. "If you'll let me continue."

She told the story, leaving nothing out. It was a long and intricate tale, but she effortlessly wove together the details. Once she was finished, she waved a hand at Ruby. "Go ahead, dear. I believe you have something to add."

Ruby nodded. "Upon a second, careful examination, I determined the cause of infection."

"What was it?" Robert asked, leaning forward.

"I found a bite mark on Donna's scalp. It was a shallow cut hidden by her hair which is why we overlooked it," Ruby said.

"Mmff," Claudia said, folding her arms. "You shouldn't have missed it in the first place."

Ruby flashed her a look. "We won't make that mistake again, I assure you."

"No, we won't," Theresa said with a decisive look. "In the future, we will be more thorough in our examinations, and something like this will never happen again."

"Yes, well. Time will tell," Claudia said, seemingly not convinced.

"We are also instituting a forty-eight-hour quarantine period for anyone who gets bitten or exhibits symptoms," Theresa continued.

"We've already outfitted one of the storerooms below. It should serve quite well," Robert said.

"Thank you, Robert," Theresa said. "The next thing on the itinerary is the newcomers. Robert, Leo, and Frank met with them this morning."

"What did they want?" James asked, leaning forward in his chair.

122

"They want cooperation," Robert said.

"Which means what exactly?" Claudia asked with a suspicious look.

"They want us to trade and to help each other in times of trouble," Robert explained.

"Trouble? Like what?" Claudia said.

"Like being overrun by a horde of zombies or being attacked by other people," Robert said.

"Other people? Why would they attack us?" Claudia asked.

"Not everyone we meet will be friendly. Some of the people we meet will want what we have, and we need to be prepared. Having an ally could help."

"That doesn't sound so bad. Being allies," Mason said.

"No, but it will require careful negotiation," Theresa said. "And we don't know if we can trust them yet."

"So, what do we do? What's the plan?" Claudia asked.

"For now, we focus on what we need to do while keeping in contact with the hospital group and getting to know them better," Theresa said.

"Yes," Robert said. "We play it safe."

"Does anyone disagree?" Theresa asked. Nobody spoke against the idea, and she nodded. "Moving on. What's next?"

"Another issue that reared its head this morning is that we can't see outside when we're in the garage. The only windows are too high up. Whenever we venture outside, we're taking a fat chance. Anything could be lurking outside, and we wouldn't know until we open the bay doors," Frank said.

"We can put someone on the upper story or the roof," Theresa said. "Like you did with Sarah and Timothy."

"Yes, but it's not enough," Frank said.

"There are windows on the ground floor. They're just too

high up to see what's outside, but if we can put up a platform for easy reach, it would solve that problem," Robert suggested.

"Good idea. Maybe one on either side of the bay doors?" Frank suggested.

Robert nodded. "We can make that happen. It shouldn't take too long to rig something like that up."

"Let's put that at the top of the list then," Theresa said, jotting it down on her clipboard. "What else?"

"It's all well and good to set up a platform in the garage, but that's kind of missing the point," Clare said.

"Which is?" Theresa asked.

"There shouldn't be any infected inside the block. That's what the barricades are for," Clare said. "Or that's what they're supposed to be there for."

"The barricades are there, but they're not foolproof," Robert said.

"Then you should make them foolproof," Sandi said, seemingly deciding to speak up.

"That's easier said than done," Robert protested.

"Get it done," Sandi said. Leaning forward, she placed both hands on the table. "The most important thing we should focus on right now is our safety. The children's safety. Especially after last night."

"She's right," Theresa said. "We can't afford to lose any more people. Three is already too many."

"What about guards?" Frank said. "I know we talked about it, but we never got around to setting up a roster."

"It'll go a long way to securing the block," Robert agreed.

"I can set up a roster, but I'll need volunteers. People who can use a rifle at a long distance with fair accuracy," Frank said.

A few hands went up: Sarah, Timothy, Ellen, Rick, Leo, and

Clare.

"What about you, Bobbi?" Theresa asked. "You're a good shot."

"Yes, but I'd prefer to take over communications," Bobbi said. "And I can look after Sebastian."

"Sounds good," Theresa said, making another note on her clipboard.

"I'll ask our people. There's bound to be someone who can use a gun," James said.

"I'm willing to learn if someone will teach me," Amelia said, raising a hand.

"It's too dangerous," Robert protested, reaching out to take her hand. "I won't have it."

"It's not up to you, sweetheart," Amelia said, standing her ground. "This is my decision, and I want to learn."

"She won't be in harm's way, Robert," Susan pointed out. "If anything, she'll be safer on the roof than down in the streets."

"Exactly," Amelia said with a look of triumph. "Plus, it will give me something to do besides twiddling my thumbs."

"Alright, but be careful," Robert said.

"Of course," Amelia said. "Now, who will teach me?"

"I will," Frank said. "As well as anyone else who wants to learn how to shoot. I've shown most of you the basics, but we should all know how to handle weapons in case of an attack."

"Maybe you and Leo could take turns giving class up on the roof," Robert suggested.

Frank nodded. "We'll put up a schedule on the notice board. If you're free, drop by."

"And I'll see what I can do about the barricades," Robert offered. "We'll probably need more material and equipment."

"That means more supply runs," Theresa said.

"I need canning and bottling supplies to store surplus food," Sarah said. "It's amazing how much people can eat."

"We should get the garden growing," Timothy said.

"What about the power? It's got to go soon, right?" Susan said. "What do we do then?"

"We've got a couple of backup generators," Robert said.

"And the gas station is part of the block now. We can get fuel there," Mason said.

"It's not enough," Susan said. "What happens when the fuel runs out?"

"Susan is right. We need to be prepared," Theresa said. "Any suggestions?"

"Solar lamps, lights, and candles for a start," Robert said. "Our kitchen has a gas stove, but we should get more for the other buildings and extra gas cylinders."

"We can install solar panels on the roof with inverters and battery banks in one of the storage rooms," Timothy said. "We've got them on the farm, and it works."

"Yes, but it's a big undertaking, and it will take time to set up," Robert said.

"We don't have a lot of time," Theresa said. "For now, let's focus on getting generators installed, here and next door. The gas station and clinic too."

"We should set up an extra space to store frozen foods with a generator to run the freezers should the power go out," Susan said. "Once the food rots, it's over."

"The supermarket," Robert said. "The small one on the other side of the block. It's already got freezers in place, and there's still some food left. We can set up a generator and add to the stock as we scavenge."

"Right," Theresa said, looking at her list. "From the top,

Frank is in charge of setting up a guard duty roster. All volunteers are to report to him directly."

"Yes, ma'am," Frank said.

"Frank and Leo will also offer lessons in gun usage and self-defense. Everyone capable of wielding a gun must report for these lessons whenever possible. Got it?"

A chorus of yesses and nods did the rounds.

"James will ask next door for volunteer guards and sign his people up for the classes as well," Frank said.

"That's right," James said. "We are happy to help."

"Thank you," Theresa said. "Is everyone satisfied? Any questions?"

As she asked the question, the power shut down, plunging them into the gloom. Theresa looked around, startled despite herself. Even though she'd expected the electricity to go, it was still a shock.

"I think our list of priorities has just shifted," Theresa said. "Robert, please put together two teams to get the generators installed and up and running. You also have to figure out a solution to the water problem."

"Yes, ma'am," Robert said.

"Frank, you and Leo can go ahead with your guard roster and training. That remains important, and having a guard on the roof will add an extra layer of defense."

"Of course, ma'am," Frank said.

"Bobbi, please remain in contact with the hospital. I would like to speak to someone in charge soon," Theresa added.

"I'll arrange something," Bobbi said.

"Susan, I'm placing you in charge of the food. Recruit whoever you need to help you store as much as possible before it goes off. We'll likely be forced to ration electricity as we can't run the generators day and night."

"I'll make a plan," Susan said.

"James, if anyone in your group has expertise regarding water, electricity, and plumbing, please have them report to Robert."

"I'll ask around," James said.

"Sandi, I trust you and the other teachers can keep the children happy and occupied?" Theresa asked, looking at the teacher.

"We can, but we could use some stationary, books, and toys," Sandi said.

"I'll add that to the scavenger list as soon as we get the water and power set up," Theresa said.

"What about me?" Claudia asked.

"Someone with as much authority and influence as yourself can help smooth the transition," Theresa said, quirking an eyebrow. "Going forward, we will have to ration our food, water, and electricity. We also can't have people running around doing their own thing. We'll schedule times for people to go outside, but until we get everything sorted, their freedom of movement is curtailed. Can you manage that?"

Claudia puffed up underneath Theresa's praise, envisioning herself as a ward to her subjects. She'd guide them along the right path and ensure the rules were followed. "Of course, I can help with that. For someone like myself, taking the reins comes naturally."

"Thank you," Theresa said, hard put not to roll her eyes. Handling people like Claudia didn't require much finesse. Just a thick slather of praise countered with the slightest suggestion of doubt.

After a final look at her list, she said, "I think that covers it.

Everybody has jobs, and if you don't know what to do with yourself, find something. In the meantime, I'll be on George duty should anyone need me."

Theresa pushed back her chair and stood up. "Oh, and besides myself, Robert is in charge of all operations. He has the final say, and if you want to know something, ask him."

After a brief farewell to everyone, she gathered her things and left the room. On the way out, she stopped next to Susan. "Can I ask you a favor?"

"Go ahead," Susan said.

"I just gave Claudia a taste of power, and it might go to her head. Please, keep an eye on her, and if she goes too far, inform Robert of myself."

"Will do," Susan said with a twinkle in her eye. "Claudia is no match for me."

"I know. That's why I asked you," Theresa said, knowing she could trust Susan to handle the situation. *I can trust all of my firefighters, and that's what makes them so special. Come rain or shine.*

Chapter 18 - Amelia

One week later...

Amelia squinted at the target through the scope lens and pulled the trigger. The barrel jerked up, and the firing pin clicked on an empty chamber. "Damn."

"You're being too hasty," Frank said. "Take your time—steady your body. Breathe out and squeeze the trigger. Don't yank it. Never yank it."

"I know; I know," Amelia said in a low whisper.

"Then do it," Frank said, his tone uncompromising. "I can see your gun jerk up from here."

"Sorry," Amelia said, turning bright red.

He nodded and continued down the line, correcting posture, giving tips, and helping his students to shoot their best. Frank was a good teacher, and many of their people were becoming decent shots under his tutelage. Both with a rifle and a handgun. All except for Amelia, who was beginning to think she was unteachable.

"All right; one more time," Frank said, and everyone took an imaginary shot.

The system wasn't perfect. They couldn't afford to waste live rounds. They only got three real bullets to test on the target at the end of the lesson. To use any more was a waste of ammunition. Frank made the best of it and taught them everything he knew.

Ten minutes passed while they tried to do everything perfectly. They were lining up, getting their balance right, breathing out, and squeezing the trigger. It was a repetitive task, but one designed to drill it into their minds and build muscle memory.

Finally, the radio at Frank's side crackled, and he answered. "Frank here. Over."

"This is Robert. We're in position. Over."

"Thanks. Commence operation. Over," Frank said.

"Got it," Robert replied. "Out."

They could hear the distant whoop of the firetrucks' alarm from their position on the roof. It called out to the nearby infected, inviting them to follow the sound. Once it faded into the distance, taking any nearby zombies with it, Frank lifted his hand in the air.

"Load," he said, and everybody loaded three live rounds into their guns.

"Ready?" he asked, waiting until everybody affirmed.

"Remember what we practiced," he added.

"Yes, Sir," everyone agreed.

"Shoot!"

The first volley rattled off.

Amelia's bullet punched into the target, right at the lowest edge. "For fuc—"

"It's okay, Amelia," Frank said. "You hit the target this time. That's progress."

"Thanks," Amelia said, but she couldn't help but notice the round hole in the forehead of Clare's target while Susan had decapitated hers. Ellen scored a shot through the heart, and James nailed his zombie in the shoulder. Even Sandi managed a hit to the chest. *Am I the only one who can't hit a stationary fucking target?*

"Ready for the next round?" Frank asked again.

"Ready," everyone said.

"Fire!"

The second bullet flew from Amelia's gun. The hole moved an inch higher, and she smothered an angry yell.

"Getting closer," Frank said in a soothing voice that grated her nerves.

Closer, my ass," she thought to herself. *I can't shoot for shit.*

"This is your last try for the day, guys. Give it your best shot," Frank said. "Ready?"

"As ready as I'll ever be," Amelia mumbled.

"Fire!"

Alright. Let's do this, Amelia thought. She focused on the target, steadied her aim, breathed out, and squeezed the trigger. The gun barked, and she blinked at the roughly drawn outline on the paper, her heart in her throat.

A neat hole had punched through the paper man's face, and Amelia stared at it with shocked surprise. I did it. I can't believe I did it.

Getting to her feet, she jumped up and down. "I did it. I damn well did it. Take that, zombie suckers!"

"Well done, Amelia," Frank said with an approving nod once he confirmed the shot. "You did well."

"Thanks," Amelia said, beaming.

"I think you might even be ready for your first guard duty assignment," Frank added.

"Really?" Amelia asked with a mixture of nervousness and

eagerness.

"Yes, I think you can handle it," Frank said. "We'll start you off with an easy shift. Say, tomorrow, late afternoon?"

"I'll be here," Amelia said, puffed up with pride.

"Excellent. Report for duty at two in the afternoon. You'll stand watch until seven," Frank said.

"I won't disappoint you," Amelia said, resisting the urge to salute. But only soldiers did that, didn't they? She wasn't sure, but the whole thing seemed terribly formal, and she felt like that warranted some kind of celebration.

"I'm sure you'll do just fine," Frank said with a hint of a smile. "See you at dinner."

"See you," Amelia said, still flying high on a cloud of euphoria. *I did it. I did it. I did it!*

Frank gathered up the guns and ammunition. They'd be locked away until the next lesson or if someone should need them for a scavenging trip. Only permanent guards wore guns the rest of the time, ready to fight should there be another emergency.

"Class dismissed," Frank said, heading back.

Amelia hung around a little longer, chatting with Sarah and Clare. "Did you see that? I got it in the head."

"See? I told you it was possible," Sarah said with a broad grin. "Anything is possible if you just put your mind to it."

"I knew you had it in you," Clare said, chucking her on the shoulder.

"We all did," Ellen said.

"If I can do it, you can," Sandi said.

"Thanks, everyone. I appreciate the support," Amelia said. "After sucking for many so days, I feel like I should get an award."

"Of course, you should," Sarah cried. "I'm sure we can set something up, right Clare?"

"Like what?" Clare said with a doubtful frown.

"We'll figure something out. Let's meet back here after dinner. Just us girls," Sarah said. "We can have a mini celebration."

"Alright, count me in," Clare said with a shrug.

"I'll be here," Sandi said. "The other teachers can cover for me with the kids for a while."

"Me too," Ellen said.

"What?" Sarah asked with mock surprise. "You'll drag yourself away from Rick to hang with us? I thought you two were joined at the hip."

"Haha, very funny," Ellen said, a blush creeping into her cheeks.

"Can you blame her? Rick's a hotty," Clare said.

"That he is," Amelia agreed, enjoying the lighthearted banter. "So is Mason, your brother."

"What? Ew, gross," Clare said with an exaggerated shudder.

"I think he's cute," Sandi said with a shy smile.

"Yeah? I suppose there's no accounting for taste," Clare said with a teasing smile. "What about you, Sarah? Are you a Rick or a Mason kind of gal?"

"Neither," Sarah said. "I think Timothy's cute. George too, but he seems emotionally unavailable."

"You noticed that?" Ellen said. "It's like he lost someone and never got over it."

"Exactly," Sarah said.

"Don't forget about Leo," Amelia said.

"Ugh, no. He's like an older brother to me," Sarah said. "And a colleague."

"Your loss," Clare said.

"Have at it," Sarah said.

"Thanks, but no thanks. I'm happily single," Clare said. "It's nice to talk about it, though. It makes me feel almost normal."

"It kinda does," Sarah agreed. "Anyhoo, we'll meet back here after dinner. See you!"

Skipping off into the sunset, Sarah went on her way. Ellen and Sandi followed, with Amelia and Clare taking up the rear.

"What are your plans for the rest of the day?" Amelia asked.

"I'm off on a run to a plant nursery with Mason, Ellen, and Rick," Clare said. "Bobbi and Timothy have a whole list of stuff they need."

"I wish you luck," Amelia said.

"Thanks. What about you?" Clare asked.

"Me? I'm due for a self-defense lesson with Leo in ten minutes," she said with a grimace.

"That bad, huh?" Clare asked. "I've been meaning to join in, but I've been too busy."

"Oh, Leo's good. Very good. And you won't be sorry, but I have just one word for you," Amelia said.

"What's that?"

"Pain," Amelia said, rubbing her sore muscles. "Lots and lots of pain."

Clare laughed. "I'll remember that, but I'd better get going. I'm already late."

She ran off, and Amelia went to the kitchen for a quick coffee. She'd need the caffeine to get her through one of Leo's tough love lessons. He did not believe in taking it easy on anyone, and a single session was enough to make her reconsider her goal of becoming a fighter. But she refused to give up. No matter how badly she sucked. *I have to do this. It's either that,*

135

or I'll always be a burden on everyone else.

Chapter 19 - Clare

Clare ran down the stairs and into the kitchen. She stopped next to the fruit bowl on the table and grabbed a shiny green apple. Tucking it into her pocket, she made her way to Theresa's office. After a soft knock on the door, she stuck her head inside. "Hello? Anyone there?"

"Hi, Clare," George replied, his voice rusty from disuse.

Clare stepped inside and looked around the room. "Where's Theresa?"

"She had to run," George said, propped up on a stack of cushions.

"And leave you alone?"

"I'm not a baby; I still have one good arm," George protested, waving the limb around. He picked up a bottle of water from a side table and took a couple of sips, he said, "See? I can take care of myself."

"Yeah, I'm sure you can," Clare said, though she doubted it. She did not like the wan expression on George's face or the grayish tone of his skin. He looked both tired and drained, not a good combination. "How do you feel?"

"Just peachy," George replied.

"Are you sleeping?"

"Yes, Mom," he said. "I'm eating my vegetables too."

Clare rolled her eyes. "I'm sorry. Would you rather I leave?"

"No, I'm sorry. It's just…."

"You don't like people feeling sorry for you," Clare said.

"Exactly."

"Well, I don't feel sorry for you at all. It was your own fault for getting bitten, you dumbass," Clare said with a broad smile.

"I was kinda dumb," George admitted.

"Kinda?" Clare asked, raising an eyebrow.

"Very dumb," George amended.

"As long as we learn from our mistakes, right?"

"Right," George said. "How are things going out there? Whenever I ask Theresa, she says, "I mustn't worry my pretty little head.""

"She's right. You're much too pretty to worry," Clare said with a chuckle.

"Come off it," George said with a growl.

"Things are going okay. We're holding the fort, and we're building it too. Everyone's pitching in," Clare said.

"I'm glad to hear it."

"You should just focus on getting better. We need more hands," Clare said.

"Don't you mean hand?"

"Glad to see your sense of humor is still intact."

"Oh, it's alive and well. How else could I survive around people like you?" George quipped.

"True," Clare admitted. "Anyway, I've got to run before Mason skins me alive. We're due for a run."

"I'll be joining you one of these days," George said.

"Promise?" Clare asked.

"Promise."

"Good. See you soon," Clare said with a wave of goodbye.

A glance at her watch had her stomach in a knot, and she tore through the kitchen and down the stairs to the bay area. Tripping over her own feet, she sprinted toward the waiting firetruck. "Wait for me!"

Mason sat behind the wheel with a thunderous look on his face. "You're late."

"Sorry, she cried, jumping into the seat behind him.

"Next time, I'm leaving you behind," Mason said.

"No, you won't. I'm your little sis," Clare said. "Besides, I checked up on George before I came here."

Mason's expression cleared. "How is he?"

"Better, but not great."

"Meaning?"

"He looks sick. Tired," Clare clarified.

"I hope he doesn't have an infection," Mason said.

"If he does, we might have to take the hospital up on their offer and send him there," Ellen said.

"Maybe, but George is tough," Clare said. "He'll make it."

"Let's hope so," Mason said, reversing out of the garage.

Ellen sat beside her, her rifle between her knees, while Rick sat next to Mason. Clare flashed them a smile while she checked her magazine. Once satisfied, she relaxed in her seat and made herself comfortable.

Clare stared at the scene around them as they rumbled out of the firehouse into the open. The block was busy, bustling with life aplenty, unlike a few days before. There was much to be done and only so many hours during the day. As such, everybody was expected to pitch in, and they did.

A group of kids walked around the block with plastic bags, picking up stray rubbish under the supervision of a teacher and an armed guard. Leo was getting ready for his self-defense lessons while Frank oversaw the operation of the barricades. Robert, Mike, and Elijah filled up fuel tanks from the underground container at the gas station, and Ruby set up shop at the clinic. James was loading full rubbish bags onto the back of a truck, and Claudia took inventory of incoming supplies on a clipboard.

It was good to know they were making progress, making her even more eager to help. Hopefully, their current run would be a success, and they could bring back more gardening supplies. It was a key ingredient to their future success. Leaning forward, she asked, "How far is the nursery from here?"

"About fifteen minutes," Mason replied.

"Is it a hot zone?"

"It's on the outskirts of town, and the area is quiet as far as I can tell," Mason said. "But we'd better be ready for anything."

"Gotcha," Clare said, drumming her fingers on her knees. She disliked inaction and wanted to get moving as soon as possible. Fifteen minutes seemed too long, and she wished it was over already.

To pass the time, she looked at the other party members. With Robert spending more time at the base, taking over the day-to-day responsibilities, Mason had stepped up as the leader of his own raiding party, consisting of the four of them: Mason, Clare, Rick, and Ellen.

They complimented each other's strengths and weaknesses and formed a cohesive unit. While Rick and Clare tended to be daredevils, charging in and asking questions later, Ellen and Mason were more cautious. They preferred to have a plan and always did a fair amount of reconnaissance before a hit.

We make a good team, Clare thought with satisfaction, knowing she could count on them to have her back. Fiddling with the knife at her hip, she waited until they reached their destination: Bloomingdale's Plant Nursery.

Mason parked the truck before the main entrance and shut off the engine. For several long minutes, he surveyed the surroundings through binoculars until Claire could no longer contain her impatience. "Well? Can we go?"

"I count three infected outside," Mason replied. He pointed at two figures shuffling around the parking lot and another stumbling up the road. "Plus four more inside."

"Four?" Ellen asked.

"The cashier behind the till, two people wandering through the aisles, and one going in circles over there," he said, pointing at a window. "Stuck in an office, maybe?"

"Seems like it," Ellen agreed.

"There could be more, but that's all I can see through the windows," Mason added.

"Alright, let's take care of the lot outside before we head inside," Rick said.

"I'll take those two," Clare said, reaching for the door handle.

"We'll take those two," Mason corrected. "Rick can take the other one, and Ellen can act as look-out."

"Ugh, fine, but move your ass," Clare said, rolling her eyes.

"Wait for me," Mason cried.

Ignoring her brother, she jumped out of the truck and into the road. Her sneaker-clad feet made barely a sound as she closed the distance between her and the two zombies milling about the lot like two drunkards on karaoke night.

They saw her coming at the last moment and growled with hungry anticipation. Their movements sped up, and they raised their arms to welcome her into their deadly embrace.

Bloodshot eyes fixed on her form, and teeth gnashed at the air.

Clare plucked the fire ax from her belt as she ran, holding it in her right hand. In her left, she carried the rifle, armed and ready to shoot. Ducking beneath the grasping fingers, she swept the gun through the air. The barrel connected with the closest infected's leg, and it fell to the ground with a thud.

While it struggled to regain its footing, Clare focused on its friend. With a wild yell, she swung the ax. The blade flashed in the light before it sunk deep into the neck. Muscles and tendons parted with a snap and the edge ground against the vertebrae in the neck. Half-decapitated, the zombie turned in circles as its head flopped around on its shoulders.

Clare yanked the ax free and jumped out of reach. Another chop was enough to send the head flying, and it smashed onto the asphalt a few feet away. A pool of clotted black blood formed underneath the skull, and the swollen tongue stuck out between the gray lips.

Pulling a face, she looked away and focused on her next adversary. The downed zombie had regained its feet and came at her with renewed determination. "Come on, zombie bait! I'm ready for you."

It snarled in answer, and bloody saliva frothed on its chin. Before she could attack, however, Mason was there. He crushed its skull like an overripe melon with a heavy overhanded blow. It burst into chunks of brain matter, blood, and bone.

Throwing her a nasty look, Mason said, "Next time, wait for me."

"I was doing fine on my own," Clare protested.

"I don't care. This is my team, and you follow my orders. Got it?" he asked.

Clare stared at him for a moment, tempted to say no, but he had a point. It was his team, and he was the leader. They'd all agreed to it, including herself. "Alright, I'm sorry. I'll listen next time."

"Good," Mason said, wiping his blade clean on the infected's shirt. He tucked it back into his belt as he strode toward Rick and Ellen, who hovered above the third zombie. It was also down on the ground, its face smashed to a pulp.

"Good job, guys," Mason said when he reached them.

"Thank Rick. He got to it first," Ellen pointed out.

"Doesn't matter," Mason said. "All that matters is that it's dead."

"Oh, it's dead alright," Rick joked, wiping blood from his face.

"What's next?" Ellen asked.

"Let's clear out the nursery, but if it gets too hairy in there, run back to the truck," Mason said. "Got it?"

"Yup," Ellen said.

"I'm ready," Rick added.

"Lead the way, Bro," Clare said with an exaggerated wave.

He glared at her, and she smothered a grin. Teasing her brother was the stuff of dreams. They'd done it all their lives, and the familiar routine soothed and invigorated her. Mason loved it just as much, even if he pretended not to. In the end, it was another strand in the rope that bound them together.

The nursery loomed in front of them, a long, low building made with rough timbers and a thatched roof. The bright afternoon sunlight shone on the white-washed walls and reflected off the large plate windows. Figures moved around inside, and it was hard to tell how many.

Pausing at the entrance, Mason tested the handle. The door

was unlocked, and he looked at each of them. "Ready?"

They nodded in turn, their sweaty palms wrapped around the handles of their weapons. Clare swallowed on the sudden knot in her throat, her stomach queasy. Suddenly, breakfast seemed like a bad idea, and she wished she hadn't eaten. Breathing through her nose, she calmed her nerves. *You can do this.*

Mason rammed the door with his shoulder, and it flung open. Hitting the wall with a bang, it attracted the attention of every infected inside the building. They turned toward the intruders and snarled. As one, they attacked, converging on the entrance from all directions.

Clare did a quick head count and quickly realized Mason had it wrong. Besides the cashier, there were at least five more zombies. Make that six.

Taking a stand, she lifted her ax and warned her fellow teammates. "We've got incoming. Around six, maybe more."

"I see them," Mason affirmed. "Rick, can you take the cashier?"

"I'm on it."

The cashier hung over the counter, reaching for them with milky pale arms. She growled with frustration, unable to climb over the barrier. Scrabbling at the smooth surface, she flopped around like a fish out of water.

Rick stepped up and dispatched her with a single mighty blow. Preferring a hammer, he hit her on the head and smashed her face into the counter. Her skull imploded with the impact, and her body spasmed with the last echoes of life.

"Done," Rick said with a grim look. He turned back in time to meet the first wave of incoming zombies, and they stood side by side to meet their foes.

Lifting her ax, Clare launched herself into the fray. She slashed at the nearest body that came her way and missed. The blade sunk deep into the flesh between the neck and shoulders. She pulled back on the handle, but the weapon stuck. With a yell, she booted the infected in the chest and wrenched the ax free.

The zombie fell back, and she took her chance. With a second blow, she caved in its skull, and it flopped to the ground. Another one stepped into the gap, and she hit it with the back end of the fire ax. The heavy metal crushed the bone and damaged the brain. With a grunt, the zombie collapsed.

Breathing hard, Clare looked around. A total of eight zombies lay on the floor, seven of them dead and another unable to stand. Stepping up, Mason put it out of its misery. It joined its brethren in final death, a sad remnant of the person it once was.

"Let's get them out of the way," Mason said, grasping the nearest corpse in a firemen's hold. He dragged it to the side and returned for another. Clare copied him, and they soon cleared the entrance of any obstacles.

"Right, let's move. You know what to do," Mason said. "I'll take gardening equipment. Rick, you're on soil, pots, and fertilizer. Ellen and Clare, you're on seed duty, and anything else you think might be useful."

"Got it," Clare said with a nod.

"Be careful. There might be more zombies around," Mason added.

"We're always careful," Clare said, rolling her eyes.

"I wasn't talking to you," Mason said, looking at Ellen. "You never listen to me anyway."

"True," Clare said with a chuckle.

She turned toward the interior of the nursery and spotted a rack filled with seed packets. Ellen found a shopping cart, and they tossed in the entire lot.

"I think this should feed us for at least a hundred years," Clare said.

"You never know," Ellen said with a grin. "Let's see what else they have."

"Ladies first," Clare said, waving a hand.

Together, they continued down the aisles, looking for anything of use. Besides seeds, they found liquid fertilizer, plant care sprays, and treatments. They also found a section filled with pet supplies, and Clare stocked up on cat food and litter for Sebastian.

"This should make Bobbi smile," she quipped.

"She can smile?" Ellen said with mock wonder.

"I've seen it happen once. It was a miracle," Clare replied.

"Ooh, look at that," Ellen said, pointing to a rack close to the cash register. It was filled with fancy treats such as organic jams, nut butter, cookies, biscuits, fruit pastilles, dried fruit, nuts, and swiss chocolate.

"Are you thinking what I'm thinking?" Clare asked, eyeing the selection.

"Party time?" Ellen said.

"You got it!"

They loaded everything into the cart and headed back to the entrance. Packed to the brim, they stored their loot inside the fire truck and went back for a second round. This time, they emptied the fridges of sodas, water, and juices and grabbed armloads of magazines. The chips and snacks rack was next, and they found a first-aid kit behind the counter. There wasn't much else of use, and they resigned themselves to a long wait.

Thankfully, Mason and Rick returned soon after that, each pushing a loaded cart.

"Did you get what you wanted?" Clare asked.

"We did. What about you?" Mason replied.

"Same here," Clare said.

"Any trouble?" Mason asked.

"Nope. You?"

"There was a terrible stink back there, and we thought it might be zombies," Rick said.

"What was it?" Ellen asked.

"Dead fish. Khoi fish," Rick said, shuddering.

"Poor things," Ellen said.

"Too bad we can't eat them," Clare said.

"Really?" Mason said, raising an eyebrow.

"What?" Clare said with a shrug. "I like fish."

"Let's go," Mason said with a sigh. "I need a break."

"From stinky fish or me?" Clare asked, following him outside.

"Both," Mason said with a groan.

Clare smothered a grin, secure in the knowledge that some things never changed, and they never would if she had her way.

Chapter 20 - Ellen

That night, Ellen couldn't wait for dinner to end. She fidgeted in her seat and jumped up the minute it was allowed. Storming back to the dorm, she removed a pack from underneath her bed. She'd stashed it there earlier, containing a selection of the treats they'd swiped from the plant nursery.

"What's that?" Rick asked, making her jump.

"Um, nothing," Ellen said with a bright smile.

"If it's nothing, why do you look so guilty?"

"I don't look guilty. Do I?" Ellen said. "Why would I look guilty?"

"You tell me," Rick said.

"Fine," Ellen said with a sigh. "It's a bag of goodies from the nursery."

"And you kept it, why?"

"Us girls are meeting on the roof for some downtime," Ellen said, "and I thought a few treats would be nice."

"I see. I take it I'm not invited," Rick said.

"Nope, but I'll make it up to you later," Ellen said, jumping up.

Rick pulled her into a deep embrace and smiled. "Promise?"

"I promise," Ellen said, granting him a long, slow kiss.

"I'm holding you to it," Rick warned as she ran off with her bag of stolen treats.

"If I don't, you can spank me," Ellen said with a wink.

"Deal!"

She made her way to the roof, where the rest already waited. "Hi, guys."

"Did you bring it?" Clare asked with a stealthy look.

"Of course I did," Ellen said, producing the bag. "Swiss chocolate, anyone?"

"You're kidding," Sarah exclaimed.

"I am not," Ellen said, producing a bar of the fine chocolate. "I also have honey nougat and caramelized nuts."

"Oh, my God! You're a star," Amelia cried, grabbing a piece of nougat. "I never thought I'd get to eat this again. Ever." She unwrapped the candy, took a bite, and groaned with pleasure. "Mm, that's so good."

"Give me some of that good stuff," Clare said, taking a piece of fudge.

"What about you, Sandi?" Ellen asked.

"Anything with caramel for me," Sandi replied.

Dishing out the sweets, Ellen took a piece of chocolate for herself and settled on a nearby bench. The rest followed, and they formed a circle of camaraderie.

"So, tell me how you met Robert, Amelia?" Clare asked.

"How we met? Gosh, that's so long ago, I forget," Amelia said.

"Come on. Dish the details," Clare prompted.

"Well, he asked me to the prom, screwed up the details, and arrived in a purple tux," Amelia said.

"Purple?" Clare laughed.

"What color was your dress?"

"Lime green," Amelia replied. "We looked like two clowns

who escaped from the circus. Despite that, he made the best of it, and I was hooked."

"That's a great story," Clare said.

"What about you?" Amelia asked. "No one special?"

"Nope. My last date puked on my new shoes and left with another girl," Clare replied.

"Her loss; your gain," Amelia said.

"I haven't had time for romance," Sarah said. "Not with the academy and training and stuff."

"Me neither. My kids are my life," Sandi said.

"Not Ellen, though," Clare said. "She'd got it going on."

"Yup, I sure do," Ellen said with a grin. "And I am not complaining."

"I'm sure you're not," Clare said. "Anyway, enough with the romance talk. Let's talk guns."

"Guns?" Sandi said, wrinkling her nose. "I'd rather not. Frank shoves it down my throat every single day."

"True," Clare said. "How about a party trick? I can bend my thumb backward."

"Prove it," Ellen said.

Clare complied, pulling her thumb back until it was level with the rest of her hand.

"That is so gross," Sarah said with a shudder.

Clare shrugged. "Maybe, but not many can do it."

"I can tell jokes," Sandi offered.

"Okay. Go ahead then," Ellen said.

"What did the fish say when he swam into a wall?" Sandi asked.

"What?" Ellen prompted.

"Dam," Sandi said, chuckling like crazy. "Dam. Get it?"

"Er. We get it," Ellen said.

"Sorry, I guess I'm not that funny," Sandi said. "The kids like my jokes."

"Yeah, I can see that," Clare said.

"It doesn't matter," Amelia said. "What matters is that we're here, alive, together, and laughing."

"Cheers to that," Sarah said, taking a big bite of chocolate. She grinned at them with choc-stained teeth, and everyone burst out laughing.

Ellen leaned back in her chair, feeling at peace for the first time in days. While she loved Rick and enjoyed every second of their fresh new relationship, it was still the apocalypse. Good people were dead, and more were dying. Humanity teetered on the brink.

But despite that, here they sat. A gaggle of women talking and having fun as if nothing had happened. For a brief period, they could set aside their differences and pain. They were able to be themselves, and that was enough.

Chapter 21 - Bobbi

Bobbi dug her hands deep into the soil and rubbed the rich matter between her fingers. It was good earth—the kind made for growing things. Flowers, fruits, vegetables, and herbs. It reminded her of her garden and the bounty she used to grow there. *With this, we can eat like kings.*

She dropped the handful of soil and formed a shallow trench with her hands. Selecting a packet of seeds, she tipped them into her hand and carefully planted a row of radishes. With the first row done, she planted a second and a third. Once the box was full, she searched for a watering can. She found one three pallets over and used it to water the freshly planted seeds.

Smiling with satisfaction, she surveyed the rooftop of the fire station. In just a week, it had changed radically. After the meeting and the loss of the power grid, everyone jumped into action. Scavenging parties went out twice a day, returning with the items they needed to set themselves up for survival: Gardening equipment, building material, food, medicine, bottled water, and furniture.

At home, teams worked to set up the generators, keep them fueled, and install water pumps, rain catchment systems, and tanks. They filled wooden containers with earth and planted winter crops on the fire station's roof.

Frank taught the untrained how to use guns, Leo taught them how to fight, and they set up a guard roster. The barricades were improved, and not a single infected had intruded into their space in a long time. Even Sebastian had settled down. He was now allowed the run of the station, and he'd quickly become a favorite with everyone. Everyone except Robert.

Bobbi choked back a laugh. Poor Robert would never get used to the feline. He just wasn't a pet person, especially cats. To make it worse, Sebastian seemed to sense his aversion and found great pleasure in taunting the man. He'd jump on the kitchen table and walk past Robert, waving his tail in his face. After waving his butthole in Robert's face, Sebastian would sit down and proceed to groom himself while staring at the man with kingly disdain. It was pretty hilarious. To Bobbi, at least.

"How's the gardening coming along?" a voice asked behind her.

She turned and spotted Amelia. "Not bad. It'll be a few weeks before we can eat any of it, though."

"I thought as much," Amelia said, inspecting the rows of boxes on the roof. She carried a rifle, and Bobbi guessed she'd volunteered for guard duty.

"How are the gun lessons going?" Bobbi asked. While Robert was not a cat person, Amelia at least tried to be nice to Sebastian despite being allergic. For that reason, Bobbi was willing to accept her, if not become best friends.

"Okay," Amelia said. After a pause, she added, "It's a lot harder than I thought it'd be, but I'm learning."

"Just keep at it. Practice makes perfect even though it gets tedious," Bobbi said.

I got my first headshot the other day," Amelia said with a

153

mixture of hope and pride.

"That's great," Bobbi said, striving to look impressed. Being a good shot herself, she didn't bother with the lessons and didn't think a headshot at a stationary target was that impressive. Especially with a scoped rifle while sitting in a supported position. But Amelia looked so happy that Bobbi couldn't bear to burst her bubble.

"Thanks. I can only get better, right?" Amelia added.

"Exactly. Do you feel ready for guard duty?" Bobbi asked.

"Not really. I probably wouldn't be able to hit the broad side of a barn with this thing, but I'm sure I can run and scream if I see something coming," Amelia said with a shrug. "I think that's why Frank gave me the afternoon shift."

Bobbi laughed. "Works for me."

"You'll be the first one I run to," Amelia said.

"Deal," Bobbi said. "Seriously, though, keep at it. You'll get the hang of things," Bobbi said.

"I'll keep practicing, but right now, I'd better go do my job," Amelia said with a wave.

"Have fun," Bobbi said, returning to her garden work.

Throughout the afternoon, she planted, watered, and weeded. The work was therapeutic, and it calmed the rough edges of her being. She'd always enjoyed gardening and had a real knack for it. Everything she touched, flourished. It was just one of her talents.

While she moved, she hummed beneath her breath, and it wasn't long before Sebastian found her. Now that he was free to roam, he spent hours exploring the station's nooks and crannies. There were many things to hold his interest, and she rarely saw him except at meal times. He never missed those.

He dropped in on her from time to time, just like now.

Staring at her with his grass-green eyes, he meowed before rubbing up against her leg. Bobbi took a few moments to scratch him behind the ears. Purring, he enjoyed the attention until he got bored. With a flick of the tail, he left, leaving her to her own devices.

Shaking her head, Bobbi watched Sebastian leave. He'd be back when he wanted more attention. Until then, he'd act like he didn't need her. Cats. You didn't own them. They owned you. She didn't mind, though. He filled the void left by the loss of her dogs, which was enough for her. That and her gardening. *As long as I have this, I can survive. I can flourish, just like my plants.*

Chapter 22 - George

George drifted in and out of consciousness, unable to control his thoughts. He viewed everything through a drug-induced haze, and the world shifted around him constantly, switching between the reality of Theresa's office and the nightmares that plagued his sleep.

The pain in his arm was always there, an ache that no amount of painkillers could treat. They only dulled the sharp edges until it became bearable. It was worse when he was awake, but at least Theresa was there. Or Susan. They were always ready with a sip of water, a cool cloth, and a kind word.

Ruby came in daily to check his vitals, clean his wound, and change the dressings, while the others would pop by with a quick word of encouragement or a treat. They were good friends, and he was fortunate to be in such fine hands.

But they weren't her.

Nikki.

With the memory of their last encounter fresh in his mind, it was impossible to forget. Like his mom used to say, "Once you let the genie out of the bottle, you can't put it back." And neither could he get rid of his guilt.

It tortured him day and night, mocking him with visions of her face, voice, and laughter. It played reruns of their happiest moments together, only to torture him with horrific nightmares when he fell asleep.

It became so bad that he refused to sleep, forcing himself to stay awake until he was bleary-eyed with exhaustion. He'd pace up and down for as long as Theresa and Ruby would allow before they chased him back to bed. They refused when he protested that he was ready to go back to work.

"You're not ready yet," Theresa said.

"I don't care," he said.

"I do. If we let you overexert yourself, you could tear out your stitches or develop a fever," Theresa said, her lips compressed into a thin line.

"Ruby?" George pleaded.

"Forget it," she said.

Sulking, George stayed in bed, but he still refused to sleep. Even when his eyes refused to stay open, he wouldn't lie down, dozing in fits and starts.

"George, you have to sleep," Ruby said, swapping out his IV bag for a fresh one.

"I can't," he said, his voice hoarse.

"You must, or you won't heal," Ruby said.

He shook his head, his lips set in a stubborn line.

Turning her back, Ruby rummaged through her kit. When she turned around, she had a syringe in her hand and injected the liquid into his IV bag.

"What's that?" George asked, suspicious.

"Just a dose of antibiotics," Ruby said.

"Uh-huh," George said, narrowing his eyes. When he felt the onset of drowsiness, he swore. "Damn it, Ruby. Why?"

"I told you. It would help if you slept, and you will," she said. "Even if I have to make you."

"No, I can't," George protested, his lids growing heavy.

Ruby paused next to him and placed a hand on his shoulder. "George, whatever demons you're running from inside your head won't go away until you face them."

"Face them," George mumbled.

"That's right. You have to face them," Ruby said, squeezing his shoulders.

As George sank into a deep sleep, he tried to remember her words. Darkness gathered around him, thick and oppressive. His heartbeat picked up, going faster and faster. The first pricklings of fear tugged at his gut, and he whirled around, looking for a way out.

Then, he saw it—a light. With a glad cry, he ran toward it, only to stumble to a halt. A familiar scene lay before him, and he frowned with confusion. A two-story house was on fire, and he stood on the pavement holding a hose. He was dressed in full turn-out gear, and the flashing lights of the firetruck lit the area with a lurid glare. *What is this? What am I doing here?*

He looked around and spotted Susan, her eyes wide with fear. Her mouth was open in a silent scream before she whirled around and ran away. "Susan? Where are you going? Come back!"

A knot of writhing figures drew his attention, and he spotted the Captain down on the ground, covered with leeches. They pinned him to the ground, sucking his blood from his veins with their slime-covered mouths. *Giant leeches? That's not possible.*

George moved closer, and his vision cleared. Not leeches. People. Crazed, cannibalistic people. Unable to believe his eyes, he dropped the hose and backed away. "Captain!"

A dozen snarling faces turned toward him, blood dripping

from their chins. They growled at him, their teeth bared, and panic spurted through his veins. Forgetting about everything, he ran.

Sprinting down the street, George pushed his body as hard as possible. His gear dragged at his limbs, and his breath sawed in and out of his lungs. A hot poker stabbed him in the ribs, and he pressed one hand to his side. Behind him, the crazies were in full pursuit, their shrieks pushing him onward despite the pain. *Don't stop. Keep moving. But what about the others? Robert, Mason, and Susan?*

Guilt tugged at his conscience and left a sour tang in his mouth. He'd left his teammates behind to die. *The captain... oh, God, the captain.*

These thoughts and many more swirled through George's mind. It was impossible to comprehend what had happened and was still happening. He chanced a glance over his shoulder, and his heart stuttered. The crazies were gaining on him. *Come on. Faster, faster!*

An ear-splitting screech caused him to stumble. A shadowy blur caught his eye before something hit him with a glancing blow. George spun wildly, flailing his arms to keep his balance. The thing that attacked him whirled about with its teeth bared. Long strands of dark hair hung across its face, and smears of red lipstick and blood marred its skin—a woman.

No, not anymore.

A thing.

A monster.

She swiped at him with her hands, her fingers arched like claws. Long crimson nails tipped each finger, eager to tear through flesh. George jumped back, and her nails raked across his stomach.

159

The others were gaining, closing the distance while he dawdled about like an idiot. Within seconds, he regained his footing and launched himself at the witch in his path. He rammed her with his shoulder, and she flew across the tar with a shriek.

Her hair flew back from her face, revealing her features, and he froze. "Nikki?"

She grinned, her teeth pointed and razor-sharp, like a shark. "Remember me, brother?"

"No, it can't be," he whispered, looking around.

She scuttled toward him on all fours, and he broke. Pelting down the street with a fresh burst of speed, he ran to get away from her monstrous figure. A chorus of cackles followed in his wake, mocking his efforts. "Run, brother. We are coming for you."

He looked around and almost fell as shock reverberated through his being. A crowd of crimson-clad Nikkis were after him, their eyes like coals of fire. They chased him with single-minded determination; clawed hands stretched out to draw him into their wicked embrace.

George pumped his arms and legs, but no matter how fast he ran, they stayed on his heels. His heart beat wildly in his chest, banging against the cage of bone that protected its fragile form. Exhaustion set in, and he knew he couldn't last much longer. *I need to hide.*

It was easier said than done. Everywhere he looked, locked doors and shuttered windows met his gaze. Not a single opportunity presented itself. He wasn't in the suburbs anymore. The shops and offices on either side were closed, their signage illuminated by the bright glow of street lamps.

With growing desperation, George cast around for a solution. The Nikkis were now so close, he almost felt their teeth cutting into his flesh. *Shit, shit, shit.*

A car drove past, its wheels screeching as it sped around the corner. George glanced at the street signs. He wasn't far from the main highway. If he could get there, he could flag down a vehicle and catch a ride.

It was worth a shot, and he changed direction, cutting across the curb and taking a sharp turn. The Nikkis followed, their taunting cries mocking him. "You can't hide from us, brother. The time has come for you to pay."

"Leave me alone," George yelled. "This isn't real. This isn't you!"

"Isn't it? Why are you running then?"

A few more cars raced past, headed for the highway. Strange faces stared at him from behind the glass windows, their eyes wide with fright. Could they see the Nikkis? Were they running from her too?

Two more blocks passed before he spotted an off-ramp to the highway. With newfound determination, George headed up the incline. His legs burned with the effort, but he reached the top. There he slowed, his eyes growing wide. "Holy shit!"

The highway was clogged with cars standing bumper to bumper. Horns blared, people screamed, and fights broke out among frustrated drivers. Whole families were crammed into the tiny metal boxes on wheels, their belongings stuffed into every nook and cranny.

Familiar howls from behind sounded, and George glanced back. The group of Nikkis had gained on him. Within seconds, they'd be on him, tearing him to shreds. His stomach churned as terror rushed through his veins, and he broke into a stumbling run. "We're coming for you, brother. There is no escape."

George weaved through the traffic, ducking around the cars, sedans, trucks, and lorries. He slid across hoods and dodged open doors with remarkable agility. It was amazing what fear could make one do.

The mob of Nikkis followed, but the sheer number of vehicles slowed them. Bit by bit, he gained a lead, and the distance between them grew.

Others weren't so lucky as the Nikkis ripped them from their seats and tore them to shreds with gleeful abandon. Screams filled the air as death washed over the stationary traffic like a tidal wave.

Relentless.

Unstoppable.

Some abandoned their cars and attempted to escape on foot. People trampled one another in their haste to flee while others hid inside their vehicles. Their efforts were futile. Glass shattered, grinning mouths slithered through the openings, and blood splattered the windows. Entire families were wiped out within seconds.

Even worse, the dead didn't stay dead for long. They stirred where they lay, limbs twitching and jaws snapping at the air like piranhas. They rose to follow the others, and the pack of Nikkis grew into a mob.

George stumbled to a stop and turned around. Horror froze him to the spot, and he watched as hundreds succumbed to the hands and teeth that tore them to shreds. The smell of blood filled his nostrils, and hopelessness rooted him to the spot. *I did this. This is my fault.*

As he stared at the destruction, he realized there was only one way to stop it. He had to give Nikki what she wanted, and that was him. Gathering up the shreds of his courage, George called out to her. "I'm sorry, Nikki. I'm sorry I left you."

"Sorry. You're sorry?" the mob of Nikkis spat, their rage palpable. "Sorry isn't good enough. You must suffer."

"Then take me. Make me suffer, but leave these people alone. They are innocent," George said. Stepping forward, he spread his arms wide. "Here I am. Take me. I deserve to die."

The mob of Nikkis paused mid-destruction, their eyes calculating. Finally, the lead Nikki bared her teeth in a wicked grin and said, "We accept your offer."

Abandoning the other people trapped on the highway, the Nikkis moved toward him. They surrounded him until she was all he could see. Everywhere he looked, it was her face he saw, her eyes, her pain.

Resigned, George waited for Nikki to kill him. He didn't want to run anymore. Didn't want to live with the guilt of what he'd done. It would be better if he died right there, a fitting punishment for his crime.

George tilted his head back and looked up at the stars. The sky was clear, and the stars shone like diamonds against the velvety black background. With his hands hanging by his sides, he waited, ready to accept his fate.

The howls and snarls grew closer, and he braced himself for the worst. It would hurt, he knew that, but he deserved no less. "I love you, Nikki. I've always loved you."

Silence fell around him, and a mild breeze tugged at his shirt. Cool fingers intertwined with his, and he looked down to find his sister gazing up at him with soft gray eyes. She smiled. "I love you too, brother, and I forgive you."

The scene faded away, replaced with snippets from their childhood. Stolen moments when they were happy. When all that mattered was that they had each other. The memories filled his heart with warmth, and he knew everything would be okay. One day, he'd see her again and ask her forgiveness. They'd be a family again.

One day.

Chapter 23 - Paisley

Paisley woke up in the middle of the night with the urgent need to pee. She debated over waking up the teacher who shared the room with her and three other girls but decided against it. Teacher Janet was a deep sleeper and often grumpy when woken up out of the blue. It was better to let her sleep.

Instead, Paisley slipped out of her bed without making a whisper of sound. She padded across the room barefoot and sneaked through the half-open door. A lamp burned in the hallway, its light there to guide people like her when it was too dark to see.

She was glad for the light. The darkness frightened her, especially now that she no longer had Oliver to comfort her. He used to tell her stories about brave knights saving beautiful princesses from the clutches of fire-breathing dragons, and she always thought he was like that: A heroic knight battling evil.

Of course, she pitied the poor dragons too. Maybe they didn't mean to hurt the princesses. Perhaps they were just lonely and wanted someone to talk to. And who better to talk to than a princess? They were kind, beautiful, intelligent, and had perfect manners. Everything that she wanted to be one day.

Paisley knew what it felt like to be lonely. Her whole family was lost to the evil that lived inside the darkness. Even brave Oliver fell prey to their bite, and without him, she was utterly alone.

Though they tried, Aunty Clare, Aunty Amelia, and Uncle Robert couldn't take the hurt away. When they were with her, Paisley was able to forget for a short time. She loved them, and she knew they cared, but it never lasted. In the end, they left, and the loneliness came back.

The teachers were nice, especially Teacher Sandi, and some of the other adults were kind too. Like Uncle James. However, she didn't like Claudia and avoided the woman at all costs. Something in the older lady's eyes reminded her of the monsters that took her family. Something hungry.

With a shiver, Paisley made her way to the bathroom. Inside, another lamp burned on a small table next to the window. Not daring to close the cubicle door, she quickly emptied her bladder. The entire time, she prayed that the monsters would stay away, and fear lay close to the surface.

Afterward, she washed her hands like Teacher Sandi had taught her to do. It was a laborious process, especially with her being so short, and she had to jump to reach the soap. Still, she persisted and rinsed the suds away with warm water. It was important to her that she did these things. It proved that she was a big girl now. *Maybe one day, I can fight the monsters and save people, just like Oliver and Uncle Robert.*

Paisley left the bathroom and headed to the bedroom she shared with the teacher and other kids. Along the way, she accidentally bumped the side table with the lamp. It rocked back and forth before tumbling to the ground. With a muffled crack, the glass shattered, oil spilled, and the flame jumped free of its glass prison.

Immediately, a blaze raced along the carpet, the dry fibers creating the perfect kindling. It crept up the nearest curtains and set them alight. The fire crackled towards the ceiling and created a raging inferno.

Wide-eyed and terrified, Paisley backed away. What had she done? No one would think she was significant or responsible now. They'd all hate her for being so stupid and destroying their home. They might even chase her away.

Paisley gasped. The thought of being thrown out with the monsters was horrifying, and her heart beat faster than a rabbit's. *No, no, no!*

Whirling around, she ran downstairs toward the supply closet that contained all the school toys, books, and stuff. She crawled into the heap of soft toys and teddy bears and hid within their comforting warmth. It was dark inside the closet, but for once, she didn't care. The adults would deal with the fire, and someone would come to rescue her, just like before. *Someone will save me, and they'll put out the fire. They always do. That's why they're firefighters.*

Chapter 24 - Robert

Robert shifted from one foot to the other and leaned against the low wall that edged the roof. The stars were out in full force, the perfect accompaniment to the new moon. It hung high above his head. A silver plate that dripped light onto the landscape below.

It was his turn to stand watch, but he wished with all his heart it wasn't. It had been a long week filled with manic activity, and he was exhausted. But he had to set an example for the rest, and that's why he stood out in the open on a piss-cold night, looking for zombies where there were none.

"I'd much rather be in bed with Amelia right now. A nice warm bed with my arms wrapped around my lovely wife," Robert said aloud. It was a sweet fantasy but far removed from reality. Sleep was still four hours away for him, and it might as well have been forty. *Kill me now.*

As if she knew how he felt, Amelia showed up on the roof moments later. She carried a steaming cup of coffee in her hands and greeted him with a kiss. "Cold, my sweet?"

"Freezing," Robert muttered. "But I feel better now that you're here."

"Ah, you always know what to say," she said, handing him the coffee. He accepted it with a grateful smile and took a few sips. The hot liquid warmed up his core, and he felt the chill recede from his bones.

"How long do you still have to go?" Amelia asked.

"About four hours. I'm here until two in the morning. Mason's supposed to relieve me then," Robert replied.

"Four hours," Amelia said with a shudder. "That's a long time."

"I know, but I'll survive," Robert said.

"I don't know how you stand it," Amelia said, stamping her feet. She rubbed her arms and tucked her hands into her armpits.

"Get into bed," Robert prompted. "There's no point in both of us freezing out here."

"Are you sure?" Amelia asked. "I can stay a bit longer."

"You've done enough already," Robert said, finishing his coffee. He handed her the empty cup and drew her into his arms. Holding her tight, he kissed the top of her head. "I love you, Amelia. Never forget that."

"I won't," Amelia said. "Not ever."

"Good," Robert said, shooing her away. "Off with you now, before you catch a cold."

"Alright, but I'll make sure the bed is nice and cozy when you get in," Amelia said, flashing him a brilliant smile across her shoulder.

"I'm counting on it," Robert said, watching her leave.

It wasn't a lie, either. Now that the kids and teachers lived next door, there was more space inside the firehouse. He and Amelia had combined their two single beds into one, and they occupied a double cubicle in the back corner of the dorm room.

It wasn't like their bedroom at home, and he longed for more privacy, but it was a lot better than sleeping on the floor next to Amelia, squeezed into a single cubicle. He could hold his wife in his arms, at least, and made full use of the opportunity. But, it was still four long hours away.

With a groan, Robert resigned himself to the wait. He stifled a yawn and walked from one end of the roof to the other to stay warm. After a few circuits, he used his rifle to scan the barricades. Nothing stirred, and he resumed his endless walking. Roughly an hour passed, and he was struggling to stay awake when he smelled it.

Smoke.

With a frown, Robert did a quick circuit of the roof, looking for the source of the smell. At first, he couldn't find it and ran toward the roof access. Abandoning his post, he went downstairs and burst into the kitchen.

Despite the late hour, Susan sat at the table and looked up in alarm. "Robert? What's wrong?"

"I smelled smoke, and I can't figure out where it's coming from," Robert said.

"Well, it's not inside the station," Susan said. "I would've smelled it."

"Then it must be outside," Robert said, running back to the roof. When he reached it, the smell was stronger. So strong that he couldn't miss it. Susan followed him to the top, and he turned to her. "It's coming from next door. Wake the others. We've got a fire on the block!"

As she turned to obey, he moved toward the office building next door. When he reached the roof's edge, he paused. Up close, the stench of burning brick and plaster singed his nostrils, and he spotted flames flickering through the windows. Faint screams reached his ears, and he knew there was no time to waste. The fire was moving fast. Too fast to gear up if he wanted to save the people inside the building.

Running as fast as possible, Robert sprinted down the stairs toward the bay area. The rest of the station was in an uproar, and he passed Theresa on the way. Pausing, he yelled, "Fire. A big one. We need all hands on deck."

Bleary-eyed and messy-haired, she nodded. "I'll see to it. Hurry!"

When Robert reached the garage, he grabbed a fire jacket and opened the doors. They lifted with a creak of protest, and a blast of icy air hit him in the face. He rushed through the opening and stormed into the night.

Already, the fire next door had grown into a monster. It blazed from the windows on the upper floors, and smoke billowed into the sky. The heat was intense, and he knew the people inside stood little chance if he didn't get them out soon.

He ran up the stairs and banged on the door. It and the security gate was locked, and he yanked at the bars with futile desperation. "Open up. Somebody, open the hell up!" Shouts and screams rang through the barrier, and he renewed his efforts. "Open up, please!"

The rattle of locks and chains sounded before the door opened wide. The terrified features of Claudia showed, gibbering like a crazy person. She clutched a bunch of keys in one hand and the neck of her robe with the other. "Help me! Please, help me!"

"Open the gate," Robert replied but ground his teeth together with frustration when she did nothing but repeat her pleas. Losing his temper, he grabbed her arm through the bars of the security gate and pried the keys from her fingers.

Shoving the first one he could find into the lock, he muttered,

"Open up, damn it. Open up." The lock stayed shut, and he tried another one—still nothing. Finally, after the fourth try, the lock sprang open. He opened the security gate and pushed past Claudia. "Wait outside."

She obeyed with a frightened squeak, tripping down the stairs in her haste to get away. Robert did not waste any time and headed inside. He paused at the bottom of the stairs to allow a flood of frightened adults and children to rush past him, all of them in a panic.

They pooled on the bottom floor, and he searched for a familiar face. When he spotted James, he yelled, "James, get these people out of here and clear of the building. Got it?"

James nodded. "This way, folks. One at a time. Don't shove. Children first."

The milling crowd calmed down and began to file out of the open front door in a single row. Once Robert was sure they'd be okay, he ran up the steps to the first landing. The fire hadn't reached that far, and he ran down the corridor. "Fire. Evacuate the building. Fire!"

A couple of doors opened, and a few confused people stumbled into the hallway. They were primarily elderly folk and slow to react. Repeating his instructions, he herded them toward the landing and down the stairs.

The entire time, he ached to go to the next floor, confident that the fire was worse up there. If anyone needed his help, that was where they'd be.

Dancing from one foot to the other, he coaxed an older woman down the steps. She moved with the speed of treacle running down the side of a cold glass, and he growled with impatience. When a familiar voice called out his name, he perked up. "Mason? I'm over here."

"Hold on!" Mason replied. Seconds later, Mason and Rick arrived at the top of the stairs dressed in full gear, gloves, and masks. "Where's the fire?"

"Top floor," Robert replied.

"Okay, I'm going up," Mason replied.

"I'm on it," Rick said, guiding the rest of the elderly folk down the stairs toward the landing where Ellen waited to receive them. Afterward, he ran back up the steps and checked the hallway and rooms for possible stragglers.

Robert saw none of that, his entire focus on Mason's back as the younger man led the way to the second and last floor. They thundered up the steps, leaping toward the top as fast as they could.

As they ran, Mason reported the situation outside to Robert. "Susan and Ellen are checking the ground floor to make sure everyone gets out. Ruby is setting up a triage station outside. Theresa is evacuating everyone from the fire station and moving them across the road while Leo and Frank are setting up guards on the perimeter."

"Good thinking," Robert said with an approving nod.

They ran upstairs and burst onto the landing but paused when fiery heat assaulted their senses. Flames ran up the walls and covered the ceiling. It seared the carpet and raced through the air ducts.

"It's too dangerous. You're not wearing your gear," Mason yelled, waving back the way they came. "Go back and get help. I'll cover this floor."

"No, I'm staying," Robert said, shaking his head. "There are too many rooms for you to check on your own, and by the time I get help, it'll be too late. Let's move!"

"Alright, fine, but be careful and stay behind me," Mason

replied. He turned toward the hallway and proceeded to open the doors on the left side. "Firefighters. Call out if you need help!"

Robert followed in his wake, checking the rooms on the other side. He raised one hand to shield his face from the heat and lifted his shirt over his mouth. With his eyes closed to slits, he tried to ignore the extreme heat. "Firefighters. Call out if you need help!"

The first room he checked was empty. So was the second. In the third room, he found a woman and child lying on the floor with damp towels over their heads. "Ma'am, you have to get out. Follow me."

"Okay," she said in a shaky but determined tone. She scooped up her child and followed Robert outside.

"Be careful," he cautioned, shielding them with his jacket. As he guided them to the exit, he silently commended her resourcefulness. Using damp cloths to protect their lungs from the extreme heat was smart and would probably save their lives. At the top of the stairs, he encountered Rick and handed them over. "Take care of them."

"Will do," Rick said, taking over.

Seconds later, Mason appeared from the heat haze with two more people in tow. He paused next to Robert. "I found three more, but they're gone. Smoke inhalation while they slept. Fifth room on the left."

Robert nodded. "I'll check the last few rooms. Get these people out."

"Be careful. I'll be right back," Mason cautioned.

Robert ran back, aware that the fire was spreading fast and time was running out. A few more minutes, and it'd all be over. He had to check the last rooms, or it would be too late. *It's now or never.*

He tried the next door, but it was locked. Kicking it open, he burst inside. A body lay on the floor, and he quickly checked for a pulse. When he found none, he swore, "Damn it."

There was too much smoke. People were being over-whelmed in their beds. Taken by the thick, acrid fumes before they could flee. Only the youngest, hardiest, or those smart enough to stay low and cover their mouths could survive.

His own lungs burned despite the shirt he held over his nose. It wouldn't be long before he felt the effects too, and he knew he needed to move fast. Not for the first time, he missed his full gear and mask.

The next room delivered a knot of frightened people, and he hustled them toward the landing. Two of them had severe trouble breathing, and he had no option but to help them down the stairs. On the ground floor, he handed them over to Ellen, and she guided them out into the fresh air.

Susan was there too, and Rick emerged from the first floor, herding a few more people ahead of him. As they ran outside, Rick said, "We'd better get out of here. She's coming down."

"No, I have to go back. I didn't get a chance to search all the rooms upstairs," Robert said.

"There's no time. This building is about to collapse," Susan yelled, grabbing his arm. "Come on!"

"There could still be people up there," Robert protested.

"If there are, they're dead already," Susan said.

Robert shook his head, but he knew it was the truth. The few survivors he and Mason had evacuated were lucky. Anyone else still left up there would be dead by now. Killed by the extreme heat and smoke.

"We have to go," Susan repeated. "The place is gonna go any

175

minute now!"

As if to prove the truth of her words, the structure groaned. The timbers creaked, and flames raced along the walls of the stairwell. The entire place was one giant tinder box waiting to go up in smoke.

Forced to leave, Robert ran out into the night. There he stopped, sucking in lungfuls of fresh air. It relieved the burn in his chest and cleared the fog in his brain. Spotting Theresa, he hurried toward her. "Is everyone out? Is everyone safe?"

"I'm not sure. I think so," she said.

"We'd better damn well make sure," Robert said, looking around. "Where's Amelia?"

"She's safe, and so is everyone else from the firehouse. I'm not sure about them," Theresa said, pointing a hand at the teachers, parents, and children from the building next door. "But we're taking a head count now."

"Good," Robert said, relieved to know his wife was safe.

"We've got bigger problems," she said, her eyes fixed on something behind him.

He turned to look, and his stomach dropped into his boots. "The firehouse."

Flames licked at the fire station's roof and raced down the walls. Within seconds, the building would be engulfed.

"The fire jumped, and without water…." Theresa shot a meaningful look at the empty fire hydrant on the pavement. With no electricity, there was no water and no way to kill the blaze.

"I can't…." Robert began, at a loss for words. "That's our home."

"I know," Theresa said with a stricken expression.

"Robert!" a voice called.

Robert turned to look and spotted Clare running toward him. "What's wrong?"

"Paisley's missing."

"What?" Robert said, his blood turning to ice. "Where was she last seen? Where's her room?"

"On the top floor, the sixth door on the right," Clare said. "She shares the room with Janet and three other girls. They're all accounted for except Paisley."

"How's that possible? Didn't they take her with them when they left?" Robert asked, angered at the sheer negligence. *How could they leave her behind?*

"They said she wasn't in the room. Bathroom, maybe?" Clare suggested, wringing her hands.

"Maybe," Robert said, staring at the burning building. Without thinking, he bolted toward it. *She's just a kid. We can't lose her. Not like this.*

"Robert, no," Theresa cried, but he ignored her. "Robert!"

He ran through the foyer and up the stairs, bursting onto the top landing only to hit a wall of heat, ten times as bad as before. The heat threatened to cook him from the inside out, and it was impossible to breathe. Smoke swirled around his form, forcing him back onto the stairs. Staring at the raging inferno, he shook his head. *Poor Paisley.*

That was the least of his problems, however. Beneath his feet, the floor shifted and groaned, a sure sign that the structural integrity was failing. He hesitated, loathe to leave Paisley to a fate worse than death, but deep down, he knew she was already dead. Nothing could survive up there for longer than a few seconds. It was simply too hot.

Still, he didn't want to give up when an innocent child's life was at stake and tried to nerve himself to go back. *Come on,*

Robert. You can do it.

"Robert, are you there?" a voice called.

Mason.

Robert went down a few steps and peered down to the lower landing. "Mason? Is that you?"

Mason waved at him from below, his visor tilted back. "We found her. We found Paisley."

"You did?"

"She was hiding on the first floor. We found her when we did a final sweep," Mason replied. "She's okay."

"Oh, thank God," Robert said, clutching the rail.

"Stop dawdling and get your ass down here," Mason said with an urgent wave.

"On my way," Robert said, relieved beyond measure.

"Hurry. This place isn't going to last much longer," Mason urged, disappearing down the steps.

Casting one last look over his shoulder, Robert turned to leave. As he set foot on the first step, the stairwell gave an ominous groan. The wood shifted, and the railing wobbled. Frozen to the spot, he prepared to run but deep down, he knew it was already too late.

The structure collapsed along with the ceiling above his head. A pit opened beneath him, and he plummeted into a deep hole amid an avalanche of rubble. Falling into oblivion, his last thought was of Amelia and how he'd never gotten to say goodbye.

Chapter 25 - Mason

Mason heard the ominous groan of the stairs and turned back in time to see the entire top section collapse. He watched with horror as his friend and mentor disappeared into a cavern filled with fire and smoke. "Robert, no!"

A wave of hot air blasted Mason off his feet, and he fell against the wall behind him. Clinging to his mask, he struggled to regain his feet. "Robert? Robert, answer me!"

Scrambling to the hole's edge, he searched for his friend, but there was nothing but a pile of burning rubble. Slabs of wood, brick, and mortar smoldered in a heap, and flames licked up the sides. It looked like the living embodiment of hell, and Robert was lost to the clutches of demonic forces.

Unable to accept the reality before him, Mason remained frozen, one hand stretched out in a futile gesture. It couldn't be. It wasn't possible. Robert had to be alive. Miraculously trapped in a pocket of cool air. Not crushed beneath a ton of fiery bricks.

But the situation was real, and the shifting floor beneath him was a testament to that fact. Flames exploded outward, and the heat seared his flesh even through the thick material of his suit. Forced to retreat, he climbed to his feet and ran down the last few stairs. When he reached the bottom, Rick, Ellen, and Susan crowded around him.

"Where's Robert?"

"What happened?"

"Are you okay?"

Mason shook his head, unable to reply, and their voices fell silent.

Finally, Susan asked, "Is he gone?"

"He's gone," Mason confirmed.

Behind him, the fire roared, and the building began its final collapse. Rick dragged him into the night with Ellen and Susan close on his heels.

Outside, they were met by a hopeful Amelia, dressed in pajamas with a smear of soot on her cheek. She stood on her toes and looked over their shoulders. "Where's Robert?"

Mason stared at her, a knot in his throat. He tried to form the words but couldn't make his lips move. His tongue felt like a stick of wood, and his brain didn't seem to function. It was all wrong. Everything was wrong.

"Mason?" Amelia asked, a note of desperation creeping into her voice. "Where's Robert?"

Mason shook his head. "I… I'm sorry."

"Sorry? Sorry for what? What's there to be sorry about?" Amelia said, shaking her head. "Robert's right behind you. I'm sure of it."

"Amelia, come with me, dear," Susan said, reaching to take her hand.

Amelia jerked away, her expression suddenly hostile. "No, don't dear me. He's there. I know he is."

Before they could react, she sprinted toward the burning building. Mason gave chase, but his heavy gear hampered him. Rick was a little faster, but she outran both of them. Just before she reached the door, the building imploded.

It folded in on itself like a black hole, and the lower windows exploded. Glass and fiery debris flew outward and peppered the sidewalk. A roar of fire followed it, and flames licked at the starry night sky.

Blasted off her feet, Amelia flew several feet through the air. Tumbling across the ground, she lay motionless in the street. Her dark hair pooled around her face, and her pajamas were stained and burnt. Blood showed in a couple of spots, and Mason feared the worst.

"Amelia, talk to me. Amelia," he said, brushing the hair back from her face. She didn't answer, and her eyes were closed tight. He felt for a pulse and, to his immense relief, found it. It was faint, but it was there. "She's still alive."

"Let me," Rick offered. He scooped her into his arms and carried her to the temporary medical station Ruby had rigged on the sidewalk. He lay her down on a stretcher and stepped back.

"I'll take it from here," Ruby said, wheeling her away.

Mason looked around with a feeling of stunned disbelief. The office block was gone, taking Robert and several other victims with it. The station burned hot and bright against the dark backdrop of the sky. Their home was going up in flames.

He looked around, taking stock of the situation. The firefighters had rushed to the office block's assistance when the fire first broke out. When the fire jumped, they evacuated the station and pulled the vehicles out of the bay area. They grabbed what equipment they could and saved what supplies they could get. The stuff lay piled in a heap on the sidewalk, a pitiful amount compared to what they'd lost. *It's all gone. Just gone.*

Not that it mattered when weighed against the loss of Robert. Grief formed inside his chest and hardened into a ball of stone. It shoved out all other emotions, and he could focus on nothing but the pain. That and anger at himself. *Why didn't I stop him? Why did I let him go back? I should've stopped him.*

Weighed down by guilt, he allowed Susan to lead him to a secluded spot. She shoved a bottle of coke into his hands. "Drink this. It will help with the shock."

"Thanks," Mason mumbled, looking around.

The scene was one of ordered chaos. With the survivors out of immediate danger, Susan, Sandi, James, Frank, and Theresa took charge. They commandeered the building across the street and herded everyone inside. Gathering what supplies they could find, they set up cots, stretchers, and mattresses with blankets and pillows. A couple of gas heaters warmed the rooms, and the kids were coaxed back to bed.

Ruby, assisted by Ellen and a couple of volunteers, treated the worst of the injured right there in the street. Once the patients were stable, James and a couple of others transferred them to the clinic.

Susan set up a coffee station on the bottom floor, with chairs and tables for the adults. There, they could grab a few minutes of rest between their work—a brief respite from the horrors of the night.

Frank dispatched fresh guards to all the barricades, anticipating an influx of zombies. The fire and smoke were sure to draw them to the block, and he knew they had to be prepared.

Theresa did what she could to keep everyone calm and lent a sympathetic ear to anyone needing to talk or vent. She also ensured that George got transferred to the clinic, along with Bobbi and Sebastian. The cat was traumatized, and Bobbi reckoned the clinic would be quieter and less disruptive.

"I'll keep an eye on George, too," she said, leading him away with one hand while carrying Sebastian's carrier in the other.

Mason watched it all unfold from a distance. It didn't feel real to him. Not even when Clare came to apologize. "I'm so sorry. I should never have told him Paisley was missing. I sent him back in there for nothing."

He stared at her, his mouth working. "It's not your fault."

"Yes, it was. I'm sorry," Clare said, wringing her hands.

"Stop," Mason said. "Just stop. I'm having a hard enough time dealing with this without dealing with your shit too."

Clare stepped back, a wounded expression on her face. "I didn't mean…."

"Just go," Mason said. "Leave me alone."

"That's enough, Mason," Theresa said sharply. She appeared next to Clare, a phantom in the gloom. "We've all lost much tonight. Your sister included."

"It's okay, Theresa. He's right," Clare said. "I have no business dumping my regrets on him. This is my fault and my burden to bear. Not his."

"That's utter nonsense," Theresa said. "Paisley was missing. A child was in danger, and Robert knew exactly what he was running into. He knew the risks, and he chose to do it anyway."

"But he died for nothing," Clare said.

"Not nothing. He died doing what he believed in—doing what he loved. Saving people," Theresa said. "He died a hero."

Mason stared at her, desperately wishing he could take her words to heart. But the fact remained that it was his fault. Not Clare's. Not Paisley's. It was his fault. If he'd run a little faster and gotten to Robert a little sooner with the news that they'd found Paisley, the man would still be alive. *He's dead because of me, and nothing will ever change that.*

Chapter 26 - Theresa

The next morning dawned cold and bright. Abandoning her warm blanket, Theresa picked her way through the debris, placing each foot with care. Bits of glass, concrete and charred timber crunched underfoot, and a thick layer of ash covered every surface. A wooden beam groaned, straining to uphold a section of the second floor. The stairs were impassible, and the ceiling gaped open to the sky. Little remained of the fire station but a gutted shell, and she could still feel the heat that emanated from the bricks.

There was even less left of the neighboring office. The roof had collapsed along with the top floor and one wall. Its bricks mingled with the station's, and it shared its tragic demise. Smoke tinged the air, and soot left a bitter tang on her tongue. "It's gone. Our home is gone."

"It's… awful," Clare replied, her skin tinged grey with ash.

"Years of service, and now this," Theresa said, her heart aching within her chest.

"We'll rebuild," Clare said with a shaky smile.

"Rebuild?" Theresa said with a shake of her head. "With what?"

"What do you mean?" Clare asked. "We have to rebuild. This is our home."

"Not this time. Many of our supplies were stored inside this building and the next, including our weapons and firefighting gear. Even the crops are gone. Without that stuff, we can't survive or defend ourselves."

"We have to," Clare protested. "We've just cleaned out the entire block. The buildings are clear of the undead. We've got the clinic and the gas station. The supermarket. Supplies. Water. Electricity. We've come so far!"

Theresa didn't reply, despair clawing at her innards.

"Please, say something," Clare said. "You always know what to do."

But Theresa had no hope to offer. No inspiring words of bravery and courage. "Not this time, Clare. I'm sorry."

Clare stared at her, her mouth working. After a moment, she turned away and joined her brother in the search for bodies. Theresa watched her go with a heavy conscience, but she didn't stop her. What was there to say, after all? *We're doomed.*

Instead, she focused on the task at hand: Salvaging what could be saved and finding the bodies of the fallen. It was a grizzly job and a personal one for the remaining firefighters.

"I found one," Mason said, dragging away a charred board.

A figure lay in a bed of ashes, the skin blackened and peeling off to reveal the charred flesh underneath.

"Is it…" Theresa asked, too scared to utter the name.

"No, it's not him," Mason said.

"Thank God," Theresa said with a mixture of guilt and relief. She knew Robert was dead. Still, she couldn't help but hope for a miracle. While finding the body would bring closure, it would also bring an end to hope.

"I can't believe this is happening," Mason muttered, his expression one of shock and despair, and who could blame him? His best friend, co-worker, and mentor was gone, taken by the very thing he'd spent his life battling: Fire.

"It'll be okay," Clare said, placing one hand on his arm. "We'll get through this."

"Nothing will ever be okay again," Mason said, shrugging her off. He stomped away, and Clare watched him go with a look of distress.

"He just needs some time," Theresa said. "He doesn't mean it."

"I know," Clare said. "This is hard on all of us."

She turned away to continue the search for bodies, and Theresa waved to a waiting group outside. "Burial!"

"Coming," a yell sounded.

Moments later, Mike and Benjamin appeared with a wheelbarrow. They loaded the corpse and wheeled it outside, covered by a thin sheet. There, the body was placed on the back of a truck with the other victims of the fire. *That makes three. Two more to go, including Robert.*

Once Mike and Benjamin disappeared from view, Theresa sighed. "Let's finish this."

"Alright, but be careful, everyone," Mason said when the structure groaned around them. A trickle of dust and mortar rained down from the upper floor, and the stairs creaked. "She's unstable."

"He's right. Be careful," Theresa echoed.

Together, they continued to work the scene. Mason and Clare found another body, which left only Robert. Despair filled Theresa's heart. They had to find him. He deserved a decent burial. It was the least they could do for him after everything.

"Robert! Has anyone found Robert?" Amelia cried, rushing

into the station. Her eyes had a wild look, and her clothes were torn. Her long dark hair tumbled down her back, streaked with ash.

"Amelia, please. Calm down," Theresa pleaded.

"How can you ask me to calm down? Robert's missing. Maybe hurt, and I need to find him," Amelia cried.

She rushed forward and began clawing her way through the burnt remnants of the building. Her nails tore, and her fingernails ripped free from their beds, but she hardly noticed.

"Amelia, your hands," Theresa said, grabbing her arm.

Amelia shrugged her off with a snarl. "Leave me be. I have to find my Robert."

Helpless, Theresa stood back and watched as Amelia continued her frantic search. "Mason, please. Get her out of here before she hurts herself."

"Come on, Amelia. We will find Robert. I promise," Mason said.

"No, leave me alone," Amelia said, struggling against his hold.

"Get Ruby to sedate her. She needs to rest," Theresa said.

Mason nodded. "I'll see to it, but don't stop looking. He must be here."

"We'll find him," Theresa assured him.

Once Mason and Amelia were gone, Theresa and Clare resumed the search. Mason rejoined them halfway through, his expression bleak.

"Amelia is resting. Ruby jabbed her," Mason said.

"Thank you," Theresa said. "She going to need us after this."

"I know," Mason said. He tossed aside a slab of concrete and dug into a pile of rubble. After an hour, Susan arrived with bottled water and handed one to each of them. "Here you go. Take a break, guys."

"Thanks," Theresa said, taking a sip. The cool liquid revived her, and she wiped her mouth with her sleeve. "I can't believe this happened. How did this happen?"

"I don't know. This is awful. Just awful," Susan said.

"It must be an accident. A candle or something?" Clare speculated. "No one would do this on purpose."

"We'll find out. I'll make sure of that," Theresa said,

Suddenly, Mason yelled out. "I found something!"

Theresa, Clare, and Susan dropped everything and rushed over. They helped Mason clear away the bricks and chunks of concrete until the body was revealed.

"No! It can't be," Mason cried, dropping to his knees. Frantically, he searched for a pulse and a heartbeat. When he found nothing, he tried to do CPR.

Clare stopped him. "Mason, no. It's too late. He's dead."

Mason sank back on his heels, and his head dropped onto his chest. "Robert."

Theresa stared at the body until it felt like her eyes would bleed. All this time, she hadn't wanted to accept the truth. She hadn't wanted to believe that it could be true. That Robert was dead. But the truth lay at her feet, covered in dust and soot.

Robert was dead.

Theresa choked back a sob and turned away. With one hand pressed to her mouth, she stumbled outside. Faces turned her way, filled with hope at first, then despair. Robert's face was plain to see in her expression.

With sagging shoulders, Mike and Benjamin headed inside to fetch the body. They carried it outside and placed it on the back of the truck with the others. With all the bodies recovered, they turned their attention to salvaging whatever they could. It wasn't much.

Theresa didn't hang around to watch. Instead, she made her way to the opposite building where they'd set up a temporary residence. Inside, it was a hive of activity, and she sought out the nearest chair to rest her weary body. People bustled around her, commanded by Frank and Leo. With Robert gone, they'd stepped up to the plate and taken over his responsibilities.

Bobbi sat in a corner with Sebastian on her lap, operating a spare radio. They'd managed to rig it up, and she resumed its operation. Sebastion had calmed down after the fire and remained tethered to Bobbi's side.

"I heard you found him?" Frank said, offering her a cup of tea. He took the chair opposite her and folded his hands.

"We did," Theresa said. She gratefully accepted the cup and took a sip. The warm liquid soothed the raw edges of her grief, and she was able to swallow her tears.

"Have you decided what to do yet?" Frank asked.

Theresa shook her head. "Honestly, I don't know. I don't have any answers."

"Well, I'm afraid our time is up," Frank said. "We have to decide, and we have to do it now."

"What do you mean?" Theresa asked, alarmed.

"I just heard back from the northern barricades," Frank said. "We are attracting unwanted attention."

Theresa jerked upright. "How many?"

"Too many," Frank said, his expression grim.

Theresa squeezed her eyes shut, at a loss. For once, she didn't know what to do. She felt lost. Hopeless. Terrified. "I'm scared, Frank. I don't know what to do."

"We can run, but running into a world full of zombies without a plan is bound to end in disaster," Frank said.

"So, what do you suggest?" Theresa asked.

"I suggest we join our friends at the hospital," Frank said.

"You think they'll take us in?" she asked.

"I don't see why not," Frank said. "We've lost a lot, but we still have much to offer. They'd be fools not to take us."

Theresa thought it over. Finally, she nodded. "Alright. Do it."

"I know it's not what you wanted, but the station is gone. It's time to cut our losses," Frank said.

"I know. Do what you have to," Theresa said.

"Thank you," Frank said, leaving her side.

After he left to make the arrangements, Theresa stared into her cup. The amber liquid was mesmerizing, and she focused on it with all her might. It was better than whatever waited outside its soothing embrace.

She knew she needed to deal with her grief and face it, but she couldn't. Not right away. She needed time, and that was the one thing they didn't have. *Just let me hide a little longer. That's all I ask.*

Chapter 27 - Frank

Once they'd confirmed with the leaders of the Virtua Willingboro Community, Frank began the arrangements for their move. He mobilized several teams and placed them in charge of specific tasks. Once they got the ball rolling, he ensured their safety during the change. With that done, he oversaw the actual relocation.

Standing on the curb, he watched as the people from the community exited their buildings. Only, they weren't buildings anymore. They were homes built over the past weeks with the survivors' blood, sweat, and tears. Places wrested away from the clutches of the undead and turned into havens for those in need.

Day by day, they'd patrolled the streets, manned the roofs, and guarded the residents. The kids had gone to school, taught by the teachers who'd survived the school fire, and Ruby had worked in the clinic while Bobbi and Timothy planted the first winter crops.

Those who were handy worked to improve the barricades, secure the buildings, and install solar power and water pumps. Generators provided electricity in the interim, running for a couple of hours per day. They kept one big generator running permanently to keep the freezers in the supermarket running, but that was a temporary measure.

Rooftop tanks watered the gardens while others worked to preserve the fresh fruit and vegetables before it all went rotten. They'd even turned one of the basements into a root cellar to store potatoes, carrots, turnips, and beets.

While the system wasn't perfect, it was better than the alternative and would improve with time. Each person had a role to play and something to offer. With the arrival of more survivors, the block would expand until, eventually, it would take over the entire city. From there, who knew what they could accomplish? At least, that was how it was supposed to be until the fire, and now it was over.

The thick column of smoke, the crackling blaze, and the noise that accompanied the fire cast a wide circle. It rippled outward, drawing the undead toward them. Even now, they thronged the northern barricades, held at bay by small teams of fighters.

They'd lose the block without more guns and ammunition to defeat the zombies. It was an untenable situation that left them with no choice but to evacuate. When the time came to leave, they'd leave through the southern barricades. They were quieter, with fewer infected blocking the way to their new home: Virtua Willingboro Hospital.

Frank sighed, knowing they had no choice, but that didn't make it any easier. Not when weighed against all the hard work they'd put in and all the lives they'd sacrificed to do it. They would take as much as possible with them, loading it onto the back of trucks and empty trailers *I can't believe it's come to this.*

Leo joined him on the sidewalk, his expression somber. "This is it. We're leaving."

"I know," Frank said.

"It's hard to take in," Leo said. "After everything we've accomplished, we're just giving up."

"We're not giving up. We're starting over," Sarah said, joining them. Though she wasn't wearing her customary smile, her head was held high, and her mouth set in a determined line.

"Do you really believe that?" Frank asked.

"I do. We lost a lot yesterday, but we still have us, and that's what matters," Sarah said. "People are what matter. Not places or things."

"You sure know how to throw a pep talk," Leo said with a wry smile.

"You should have seen me as a cheerleader," Sarah said.

"A cheerleader? You?" Frank said with a raised eyebrow. "Why am I not surprised?

"We all have our secrets," Sarah said with a wink. "Anyway, I said I'd help with the kids, so I'm off. Try not to be so glum. Things will look up."

Sarah hurried toward the row of waiting buses, trucks, and vehicles. There, she joined a group of parents and teachers as they loaded their belongings into the baggage compartments.

"You know," Leo said, placing his hands on his hips. "I used to think she was annoying. Always cheerful, always smiling, never letting anything get her down. A really, really bright little ray of sunshine."

"I still think she's annoying," Frank said.

Leo snorted. "Admit it. You like her. You know you do."

"What can I say? She grew on me… like a fungus," Frank said with a shrug.

"You and me both," Leo said. "Anyway, she's right about one thing. We can't give up. This is a setback. Not the end."

"But we lost so much," Frank said, looking around.

"Not everything. We still have them," Leo said, pointing to a gaggle of kids leaving a nearby building.

Frank watched as the children trooped toward a yellow school bus. They were dressed in their warmest clothes, and each carried a bag filled with their favorite toys and a packed lunch for the road. They seemed unaware of the gravity of the situation, jostling for space, giggling, and playing. To them, it was all great fun—a grand adventure.

Their laughter carried across the distance, and it warmed his heart. It filled the void created by the devastation they'd suffered and gave him hope for the future. Hope for a younger, stronger generation that could march into the future and defeat the infection. Maybe the apocalypse wasn't the end but a new beginning for humanity—a second chance to get it right.

Chapter 28 - Timothy

Timothy leaned his rifle against the wall and flexed his arms and back. After three hours of taking potshots at unlucky zombies, his muscles were stiff, and fatigue had set in. With a groan, he rolled his shoulders and wiggled his fingers. Taking a quick sip of water, he sighed. "That's better."

However, a quick break was all he could afford, and he quickly settled back into position. Through his rifle scope, he scanned the barricade and looked for stragglers. He spotted one, flailing its arms and legs as it climbed over the barrier. Zooming in on its head, he pulled the trigger, and its skull exploded like an overripe watermelon. Sunlight glinted on the splattered blood and brains, and he grinned. "Gotcha."

He moved on to the next one, a crawler making its way underneath the barricade. Its head popped up next to a tire, but a single bullet from the high-powered rifle blasted it to smithereens.

It was Timothy's job to keep the zombies from sneaking up on Mason's team and taking them by surprise. Not that they needed much help. They fought like lions; their ax blades flashed in the sun as they hacked and slashed through the undead ranks.

Alongside Mason fought Clare, Ellen, and Rick. The four

formed a formidable force. The constant scavenger runs had honed their instincts and fighting skills. They were a powerful unit and a dangerous one to zombies.

Timothy took out a few more infected, clearing the area around the northeast barricade before checking to the northwest. It was farther away and technically not his problem. James from next door covered it, a decent shot in his own right.

Timothy was curious, however, and checked up on the ground team that fought to keep the infected at bay. That unit was led by Elijah. After the loss of Robert, he'd stepped up to the plate as a leader, and Benjamin and Mike formed part of his group. They were doing a good job of it, killing zombies by the dozen.

The other two barricades were guarded by two-person teams. They were much quieter with only the occasional zombie intruder drawn to the movement and noise. For that reason, they'd serve as their escape routes, with the community splitting in two.

One convoy would leave through the southeastern gate, and the other would use the southwestern. From there, they'd make their way to the hospital via circuitous routes so as not to draw the infected toward their new home.

In the meantime, Timothy, James, and the two ground teams would keep the northern barricades from being overrun. Once the block was empty, they'd make a run for it. It was a simple plan, and he hoped it worked. Knowing their luck, though, he was prepared for the worst.

After reassuring himself that the other barricades were holding, he turned his sights back to his job and took out a few more enterprising zombies. They never ceased to amaze him with their sheer stupidity, wandering straight into an ambush without a single thought. The sight of their fellow infected falling to the ground, their brains blown to bits, didn't deter them in the least. Shaking his head, he muttered, "Dumb asses."

At his waist, his radio crackled, the lines busy with chatter. He was glad, for it kept him in the loop on what was happening below. With his eyes on the ground and his ears perked for news, he waited.

"Frank? Are you there? It's Theresa. Over," Theresa said.

"Go ahead, Theresa. I'm listening. Over."

"The children are all accounted for, loaded on the bus, and ready to leave. Over."

"What about their things? Over."

"Loaded into the baggage compartment. Over."

"The driver? Is she ready? Over."

"Claudia? She says she can handle the bus. Let's hope she's telling the truth. Over."

"You and me both. What about the rest of them? Over."

"Two teachers are on the bus to keep order, and Sarah will act as their armed guard. The rest are in the truck behind the bus with their stuff, and one of the men is driving. Jones, I think. Over."

"Good. Leo will escort them in his squad car when the time comes. Over," Frank said.

"What about you? How far are you? Over," Theresa said.

"We are almost done with the loading. Most buildings have been stripped of anything valuable, including the clinic, and we filled up all the fuel tanks. We can come back for more later, but we took what we could for now. Over."

"How long before we can leave? Over," Theresa asked.

"Twenty minutes. Maybe thirty tops. Over," Frank replied.

"Thanks. Keep me posted," Theresa said. "Out."

Twenty minutes, Timothy thought. Things are moving fast. *I'd better be ready to move soon. The last thing I need is to be left behind.*

The mere thought made his stomach churn, and he quickly retraced his steps in his mind. Once everyone left, the two groups at the northern barricade would fall back. James and Timothy would wait as long as possible, giving them a head start. *Then, we'll make a run for it and join them below. After that, it's smooth sailing.*

It sounded easy enough, and he reassured himself that everything would go according to plan. The distance to the fire truck was a short sprint for him and James. Much quicker than the half-a-block the two ground teams had to cover. If anyone were being left behind, it'd be them. Not that he'd do such a thing. It was unthinkable. Chasing the awful thought away, he chastised himself. *This is going to work. Calm down, and focus on your job.*

Twenty-five minutes later, the radio at his belt crackled.

"Elijah, Mason, this is Frank. Get ready to run. We are leaving in five minutes. Over," Frank said.

"Copy that," Elijah said. "Over."

"Got it. Over," Mason said.

"James, Timothy. You know what to do. Over," Frank said.

"Yes, Sir," Timothy said, forgetting to say out as usual. Radio speak wasn't really his thing. While they'd used it on the farm where he grew up, it was without the formalities.

"I'm ready, Sir. Over," James said.

"Er, sorry. Out," Timothy said.

"Good luck, guys. See you on the other side. Out," Frank said, a hint of amusement in his voice.

Timothy renewed his vigil, the scope of his rifle pressed to his eye. Behind him, the two convoys rumbled to life. The guards at the southern barricades opened up, and the trucks, busses, and cars rolled through the gates. Once the last vehicle had gone, Elijah and Mason made their moves.

Abandoning their spots, they ran back to a single waiting truck, fueled and ready to go. Behind them, the shrieks and howls of the infected rose into the air until they formed one chaotic hunting cry. Swarming across the barrier, they gave chase.

Timothy made every shot count, gunning down as many as he could. Because running targets were nearly impossible to hit, he aimed for the chest. While the bullets wouldn't kill them, they slowed them down enough for the fleeing humans to make good their escape. A cartoon of hamburgers on legs running from rabid people flashed into his mind, and he choked back a laugh. *I must be going crazy.*

Timothy abandoned his post when he was confident his friends were safe. He raced across the roof, his movements echoed by James two buildings down. Slamming open the door, he ran down the stairs two at a time.

At the bottom, he paused to get his bearings. It was a strange building, after all. Not the station he knew almost as well as the back of his hand. With his heart slamming against his ribs, Timothy continued through the strange hallways and rooms, through the foyer, and toward the front entrance.

Slamming against the door, he burst into the street in time to see the others coming around the corner. Mason waved at him. "Get into the damn truck!"

Timothy nodded and ran to the vehicle. Jumping behind the wheel, he started the engine. He stared over his shoulder, cheering the others on. "Come on, come on!"

Seconds later, James jumped into the cab, his face flushed with the effort. "I... am not... that young or fit anymore. It feels like I'm having a heart attack."

"Yeah, well. Lucky for you, we're heading to a hospital," Timothy said as the others piled into the truck. He jammed his foot onto the gas, and they raced down the street with a squeal of burning rubber. Racing through the southeastern barricade, they headed toward their destination.

Timothy watched as the mob of infected in their rearview mirror faded into the distance. Fresh scenery flashed past his window, and he heaved a sigh of relief. It was over. As much as he hated to leave, their time at the station was done. It was time to start their new lives in their new home: Virtua Willingboro Hospital.

Epilogue I - Amelia

Amelia stared out of the ambulance's back window, watching the place that had been their home for the past few weeks recede into the distance. With it, she left her heart and her love: Robert. He was dead, crushed by burning debris, or so everyone told her. She didn't believe them. Didn't want to believe them. Refused to believe them.

How could she? The moment she allowed herself to accept everyone's ridiculous assertions that her husband was gone, she'd lose the last bit of hope that still lived inside her heart. That final spark that kept her from falling into the abyss forever. She held onto it with fierce desperation while she allowed everything else to fall away. Her life. Her sanity. Her freedom.

Looking down at her hands, she frowned. They were covered in bandages. Pristine strips of white cloth that hid the cuts, scrapes, blisters, and missing fingernails from view. They were ugly, after all—the injuries she'd acquired trying to dig through the ruins for Robert.

The bandages were there to sanitize and protect. To soothe and heal. But also to hide. Nobody wanted to see the hideous truth, after all.

Just like the wounds on her heart. Nobody wanted to see

them. They were too raw and visceral. A painful reminder of everything they'd lost in the fire. Not just Robert but their home. Their shelter. Their hope of survival.

Hiding her grief wasn't as easy as slapping a bandaid on it. That's what the drugs were for. They numbed her brain, turned her thoughts to mush, and left her a zombified version of herself.

Zombie Amelia was easier to handle than Hysterical Amelia. Nobody wanted to deal with that Amelia. A crying, screaming wreck of a woman who cared not a whit what happened to her or anyone else around her. *I suppose I can't blame them. I wouldn't want to deal with me, either.*

It was a sobering thought, but it also led to another one. *I can't leave. Not without Robert. He's not dead. He can't be.*

"Ruby," Amelia said, blinking at the figure of Ruby sitting on the opposite bench. The woman was hazy, thanks to the meds. A wavering mirage. Was she even real? That question was answered when Ruby replied.

"Yes, Amelia? Do you need anything?" Ruby asked with a look of concern.

"I need to see Robert," Amelia insisted.

"Amelia, we've been over this," Ruby said with a sigh.

"Yes, I know, and I don't believe you," Amelia said, clinging to her last shreds of hope.

"Amelia, please. Robert is—"

"No, he's not. He's alive. I know it. I feel it!" Amelia said, thumping her chest with one fist. "He's in here. Alive."

"Amelia, be reasonable. We all saw his body. We pulled him out of the wreckage," Ruby said. "And please stop doing that. You'll pop your blisters."

Amelia bit down on one bandaged hand and screamed

through the thick cloth. "I don't fucking care! Can't you understand that?"

Ruby's face crumpled up, tears glittering on the eyelids. "I'm so sorry. I can't imagine how you must feel. Tell me how I can help you?"

"I already told you," Amelia cried.

"Show her the body," Bobbi said from her seat in the corner. She smoothed one hand over Sebastian's ruffled fur, calming the agitated feline.

Amelia stared at the cat, intrigued by its princely demeanor. She didn't go any closer, however. The last thing she wanted was a swollen nose and a bout of intense sneezing. *Damned hay fever.*

Then she focused on Bobbi. "The body? You have it?"

"Yes, we do, and we can show it to you," Bobbi said.

"What? No! We can't do that," Ruby said, looking shocked.

"Why not? If she sees it, she might finally believe it," Bobbi asserted. "Besides, she's upsetting Sebastian, and he's been through enough already."

"But… they've been buried already," Ruby said. "Cremated."

"You burned him?" Amelia said, momentarily stunned. But the moment passed, and she shook her head. "It doesn't matter. It wasn't him. Robert is still back there. Injured, maybe, but alive."

"Not yet," Bobbi said. "They're on their way to the burial site now. We can still make it."

"Do you think so?" Ruby asked.

"I know so," Bobbi said. "It's the only way she'll let go."

"Hey, I'm right here, you know," Amelia protested, but shrugged when neither Ruby nor Bobbi responded. "Whatever."

"Alright. Let's do this," Ruby said, calling to her husband Elijah behind the wheel.

"Darling, listen up. We're making a brief detour."

"What? Why?" Elijah asked.

"To say goodbye," Ruby said, flashing Amelia a sympathetic look. At Elijah's quizzical gaze, she explained the situation, and he agreed. "Fine, I'll take us there. Hold on."

Picking up the radio, Elijah spoke to Frank at the head of the convoy. After some back and forth, he received confirmation and glanced over his shoulder. "Okay, we've been given the go-ahead."

"Thanks, babe," Ruby said.

"Finally. You should've done this the moment you found him," Bobbi said, flashing Ruby a look.

"I thought it would make things worse," Ruby protested.

"Worse than this?" Bobbi asked, waving a hand at Amelia.

"Yes, worse!"

"Ugh. Don't be stupid," Bobbi said, tucking Sebastian back into his carrier. The cat went willingly, eager to escape the bickering.

Amelia ignored them, watching as Elijah turned off the road to follow another truck with a tarpaulin-covered load. She stared at the plastic cover, wondering at its contents. She surmised it was the bodies of the fallen but still refused to believe that Robert was one of them. It was all a terrible misunderstanding.

A few minutes later, they reached their destination. It wasn't much—just a rough empty square of concrete surrounded by abandoned buildings. A few infected shuffled around in the distance, but they were too far away to be much of a threat. Nonetheless, Mike jumped out the minute the truck stopped and stood guard with a rifle.

Elijah parked next to them, and Ruby jumped out the back, followed by Bobbi. Amelia followed slowly, her legs wobbly from all the drugs in her veins. Nonetheless, she was eager to prove them all wrong and stumbled toward the tarp.

"Amelia, wait!" Ruby cried.

Amelia ignored her and latched onto the edge of the plastic covering. She yanked it aside, and the tarp whipped to the ground, exposing five bodies. They lay in the back, their flesh burnt, charred, and blistered. The smell of cooked flesh made her gag, but she fought the sensation and focused on the corpses.

Her eyes flashed from one to the next, noticing each one's features with minute intensity. None of them looked familiar, and one was so severely burned the face was mostly unrecognizable. Hope rose with each person she studied, and she almost wanted to laugh. "See? He's not here, Rub—"

Her voice faltered, dying on the last syllable. Her lips quivered, and her eyes burned. "R... Robert?"

Shaking her head, Amelia backed away. "No. It can't be. You're not dead; you're...."

Soot marred his skin, and blisters covered his right hand, but other than that, he looked like he always had. Like Robert. Her Robert.

But it wasn't real. He was dead. Nothing remained behind the once familiar gray eyes that stared at her, unblinking. The life that previously animated them was gone. He was nothing but an empty shell—a body without a soul.

Amelia's hands dropped to her sides, and her knees wavered. This time, it wasn't the drugs that made her feel weak. It was her heart. An empty void opened inside her chest, and darkness sucked her into its hungry maw. She welcomed it, her consciousness fading. As she fell to the ground, two words fell from her lips. *A final whisper. Goodbye, Robert.*

Epilogue II - Banks

Banks watched as the convoy from the fire station drove through the gates. Two fire trucks, an ambulance, and several other vehicles made up the group—a sizeable chunk of machinery and people. They entered the hospital grounds one by one, filled with strange faces. Faces he didn't know. Faces he didn't trust.

Lieutenant Kingsley operated the fifty caliber while his team patrolled the street outside. Ambo 22 was fueled and ready to draw away any zombies who might arrive to spoil the party. Another group of armed men greeted the new arrivals, waving them to an empty lot while volunteers waited to show them to their quarters.

Inside the hospital, chaos ruled. The arrival of the refugees had sent everyone into a tizzy, and frantic preparations were underway. Delicious smells wafted from the kitchens where a feast was underway, and a children's ward filled with toys and activities had been prepared for the kids. Rooms were readied, stores emptied, and beds set aside in the trauma ward for the injured.

It was unnecessary, in his opinion. A waste of time, resources, and energy. Once the strangers moved in, everything would change. Nothing would be the same again. Shaking his head, he said, "I don't like this."

"I know," Zoey said. "You don't like change."

"I don't like trouble either," Banks said.

"This doesn't necessarily mean trouble," Zoey said, placing a gentle hand on his arm.

"How do you know?"

"I have faith," Zoey said.

"Faith? I don't believe in God," Banks said.

"I meant, I have faith in us. In humanity," Zoey said.

"Then you're dumb. Dumb and naive."

"Maybe, but that's better than being bitter and cynical."

"You think I'm bitter?" Banks asked with a frown.

"A little," Zoey said. "And you're very cynical, but you're also a good man with a loving heart."

Banks snorted. "Yeah, right."

"It's true. I've seen it," Zoey said, nudging him with her shoulder. "Now, let's go meet the newcomers."

"I don't want to," Banks said.

"I know. We'll start small. You've already met Robert, Frank, and Leo, right?"

"Right."

"We'll start with one of them and work our way up," Zoey said.

Banks sighed. "If you insist."

"I do," Zoey said. "In time, you'll thank me for it."

"I doubt that," Banks said, but he allowed her to lead him toward the hospital where the refugees from the firehouse queued for help.

As the children lined up, clutching their meager belongings, looking scared and vulnerable, something inside him softened. Maybe this wasn't such a waste of resources, after all. Maybe he could get used to his new neighbors. They were people, after all. Real people. Unlike the monsters that waited outside. Hungry. Ravenous.

Zoey was right. He had grown bitter and cynical. After everything that had happened, he'd lost his way. It was time to have a little faith. Faith in humanity, but most of all, faith in himself.

Epilogue II - Nikki

Nikki sat at the kitchen counter, her bloody hands lying in her lap. More blood smeared the front of her t-shirt and splattered her jeans. On the counter lay a knife, the blade stained with crimson. At her feet lay a body—the body of her stepfather.

Stepfather. What a joke. More like step monster, Nikki thought, flashing the corpse a hateful glare. Grabbing the knife, she jumped off the chair and repeatedly kicked him in the ribs as her anger turned into a vicious rage. "Take that, you piece of shit!"

The body rolled back and forth with the force of her blows but settled back into its former position when she stopped. His bloated stomach hung over his jeans, his t-shirt stretched tight across his pudgy arms and chest. Slack jowls and empty eyes dominated his features, and she knew it was over. After years of wishing, it finally happened. Rex Fisher was dead.

It was hard to believe it was real. The apocalypse, zombies… all of it. At first, she'd thought he was drunk. He'd stumbled about the house, breaking stuff and bellowing like a stuck pig. Just like he usually did. It was nothing out of the ordinary.

Until he died and came back to life, gnashing his teeth like a starving animal. He'd chased her around the kitchen, desperate to get his claws on her. She'd sprinted around the table, her heart leaping in her chest like a frightened rabbit. His snarls made her stomach churn, and fear left a bitter taste in her mouth.

Then she spotted the carving knife with its gleaming edge, and hope granted her a burst of courage. She gripped the handle and spun around, her insides quailing.

Rex launched at her with a vicious grin, his bulk steamrolling through the narrow space. Chairs and cutlery went flying, and she almost lost her nerve. Somehow, she managed to stand her ground, the knife gripped in one sweaty palm.

As Rex closed in, she remembered everything he'd done to her over the years. The mental and physical abuse that left scars on her body and her soul. Once again, she tasted the fear and felt the pain he'd inflicted—the hurt and humiliation.

Hot blood rushed to her cheeks, and searing rage pushed all thoughts of fleeing from her mind. All she felt was hatred, all-consuming hatred. *I'm not running. Not this time. No more cowering. No more hiding.*

Baring her teeth, Nikki snarled back at her nemesis and screamed. "Come on, you piece of shit. Come on!"

Rex reached for her with both hands, and she ducked underneath his beefy arms. Stepping to the side, she stabbed him with the knife. The blade sank into his neck, and clotted blood spurted from the wound in thick globs of black goo.

Stumbling back, Nikki waited for Rex to go down, but he never faltered. Whirling around, he came at her again, and she scurried backward. Terror pulsed through her veins, and she narrowly avoided his grasping fingers. Ducking around the counter, she yanked open the drawer and grabbed the first thing she got hold of—a steak knife.

Compared to the previous knife, the steak knife looked like

a toothpick. Swallowing hard, she wracked her brain for a plan but came up empty. When Rex came at her again, she fell to the ground and scrambled underneath the kitchen table on all fours.

Rex followed, and one hand closed around her ankle. He pulled her toward him, and his teeth closed on her ankle with crushing force. Pain lanced up her leg, and she lashed out with the other foot. Her heel caught him on the nose, and it broke with an audible crunch, freeing her from his grip.

Nikki tucked in her legs and lashed out at Rex's face with her knife. He lunged forward at the same time, and she hit him in the eye by some stroke of luck. The point of the blade sank into the socket and penetrated the brain. Rex stiffened, and his mouth yawned open. Expelling a foul breath, he slumped to the floor. Dead.

Nikki stared at him for a few seconds before reality sank in. Black blood pooled on the floor, creeping toward her like tendrils of death. Repulsed, she got out from underneath the table and got to her feet, still holding the knife.

Her ankle burned where he'd bitten her, and the realization that she might be infected was enough to fill her with dread. With trembling fingers, she inspected the site. Purple teeth marks marred the smooth flesh, but to her relief, the thick material of her jeans had protected her flesh, and the skin was unbroken. *Shit, that was close.*

Her legs shook with shock and horror, and she sank down on the nearest chair. The knife clattered to the counter, and she stared at her bloody hands for an eternity. Finally, she realized she had to move and got to her feet.

She'd heard the rumors flying about zombies flying over the internet. She'd read the posts, watched the reels and videos.

None of it had seemed real until now. Rex had revealed the truth to her.

Nikki supposed she should be grateful. Now that she knew what was happening, she could prepare. *I can't stay here. It's not safe.*

That thought raised another question. Where would it be safe? She didn't know. Not that it mattered. What mattered was that she was free from the clutches of Rex. Free to do what she wanted, and she wanted only one thing: To find George and tell him how much she hated him.

Now that she had a mission, Nikki set about making her preparations. Her stepfather's blood was making her nauseous, and she longed to scrub him from her skin until nothing remained. After making sure the doors were locked and the windows closed and shuttered, she made her way to the bathroom.

There, she stripped off her bloody clothes and climbed into the shower. The hot water flowed across her skin and washed away the day's filth. She tipped back her head, closed her eyes, and let the water drown out the world. It disappeared in a haze of liquid that muffled all thought and sound. Warm. Soothing. Comforting. Everything her life had never been.

She stood like that for a long time before she could summon the will to move. Only when the water heater began to run dry did she grab a bar of soap and wash the blood from her hands. Afterward, she shampooed and conditioned her hair before rinsing herself off in the lukewarm stream.

With vigorous movements, Nikki dried her skin and wrapped her hair in a towel. She chose her clothes with care, picking an outfit that was comfortable, practical, and sturdy. Sports underwear, cotton socks, jeans, t-shirt, jersey, jacket, sneakers, scarf, and gloves. Her thick hair went into a ponytail which she tucked underneath a woolen beanie.

Into a backpack, she tossed extra underwear, socks, and t-shirts. She also threw in a toiletry bag with the basics, a towel, and a framed photo of her, George and their mother. It was the only sentimental thing she possessed, and she couldn't bear to leave it behind, no matter how much she hated him. It reminded her of the bond they used to have before it all went to hell. *Story of my life.*

In the hallway closet, she found an ancient bedroll and tied it to the bottom of her pack. She also took a bottle of water, a can opener, a cup, a bowl, a teaspoon, a knife, a fork, and a few cans of peaches. There wasn't much else in the house to eat, and the only medicine was a couple of bandages and a bottle of painkillers.

From her stepfather's safe, she took his gun, a Glock 17, and threaded the holster onto her belt. It was fully loaded, carried seventeen shots, and had little recoil. She knew that because George had shown her how to use it a few times. He'd also told her where Rex hid the keys to the safe. He'd wanted her to have the means to defend herself should she need it, which she found ironic since he'd left her at the mercy of a monster.

Grabbing the keys to Rex's truck, she emptied his wallet and stuffed the cash into her pocket. She didn't know if there would be any use for it but took it anyway. In the garage, she found a hammer with a decent grip and added that to her belt. She tossed her backpack into the cab and checked the street outside.

The neighborhood was eerily quiet. Devoid of the usual characters that made up the scene. There were a few signs of life. A skinny dog ran past, its tail tucked between its legs. A car stood parked in a driveway, its trunk open and loaded with suitcases. A shopping cart filled with odds and ends stood in the middle of the road, abandoned by its owner, the friendly neighborhood bum.

Deciding that she'd never get a better opportunity, Nikki opened the gate and climbed into the truck. She started the engine and reversed out of the driveway, ensuring her doors were locked and the windows closed. *No zombies are getting the jump on me.*

With the heater on full blast, she headed down the highway. Though she'd never contacted George, she had listened to the voice messages he'd left her from time to time. They were always the same. He'd beg her forgiveness for leaving her and repeat his promise to fetch her when she was eighteen. *What a bunch of crap. He doesn't deserve my forgiveness.*

But he did deserve to know what he'd done to her, what Rex had done to her, and that was where his messages came in handy. While she didn't care for his useless pleas, he always told her where he was, and according to the last note, he was in Burlington, New Jersey.

She wasn't sure what to do when she found him, but it didn't matter. All that mattered was seeing him. If the zombies hadn't gotten to him first, though, she knew that wasn't the case. He was still alive. She felt it in her gut. They were linked, after all. Bonded by blood.

As she drove, Nikki lifted her head and smiled. The freedom of the road was intoxicating, and she could feel the adrenalin pumping through her veins. She no longer had to cower under her stepfather's fist or suffer through his drunken rages. She was free, and no one could stop her.

With the coming of the apocalypse, the government was

gone. No more social services, case workers, or cops. While they were well-meaning, they were not the solution to her problem. Funnily enough, zombies were. Because of them, Rex was dead, and she was on her way to her brother. After six long years, she'd finally be able to confront him.

I'm coming for you, brother, and nothing on earth, heaven, or hell can stop me.

The End

Read further for a sneak peek at some of my other apocalyptic books, and continue the adventure.

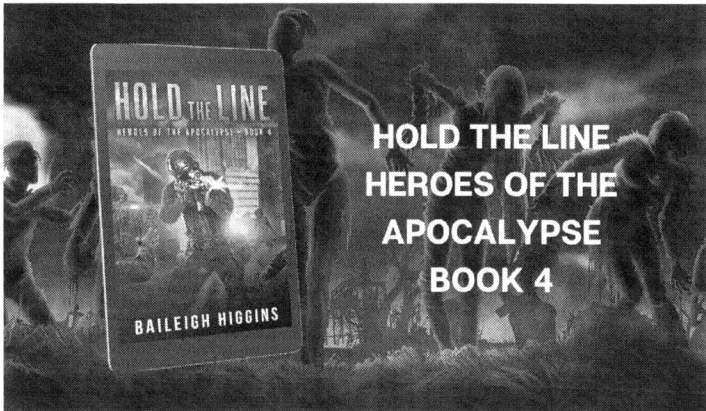

Do you want more?

So we've reached the end of Wake the Dead, and I really hope you enjoyed reading the book as much as I enjoyed writing it. If you did, please consider leaving a review. It would be much appreciated.

Plus, I've included a sneak peek at the next book in the series, Hold the Line - Heroes of the Apocalypse, Book 4. Continue the adventure! https://www.amazon.com/dp/B0B6J2553H

Prologue I - Theresa

Theresa's stomach rolled as they drove through the gates of the Virtua Willingboro Hospital. A huge gun guarded the gates, flanked by two watch towers and armed security guards. They were dressed in full gear and carried rifles, sidearms, and knives. Their gear resembled that of a SWAT team, and she guessed it was the SCERT team Frank told her about. More guards, probably civilians, patrolled the walls, but they wore ordinary clothing.

An ambulance stood to the side, waiting to lure away any unwelcome visitors from the gates. It spoke well for the place's safety, but she couldn't help but feel intimidated. Especially when the monstrosity briefly pointed at her. It was a relief when it turned back to the street again.

Scraping together her courage, she prepared to meet the leaders of the community, Sophia Ward, the hospital director, and Lt. Kingsley, the man in charge of the SCERT team, before the others arrived. She'd spoken to both in a brief conversation on the radio earlier that day, but most of the communication had passed between them and Frank.

After the fire, Frank stepped up to fill the void left by Robert and became Theresa's second-in-command. Shell-shocked by their losses, she'd let him handle most of the evacuation, a task he'd performed with admirable efficiency. *I don't think I could've done it. I hurt too much, and it clouded my vision.*

She still hurt. There was a hole in her heart where Robert's presence used to be. They'd been colleagues for years, and they'd grown close over time. After the apocalypse, that didn't change. Instead, they became even better friends, working together to save what they could from the horrors of the undead. Together, they'd shared victories, losses, and triumphs. Losing him was unthinkable, yet it happened.

In the ambulance behind Theresa's truck lay Amelia. Supervised by Ruby, she was under heavy sedation. Though it wasn't ideal, they had no choice. They couldn't afford to have her alert the undead or trust her not to do something stupid.

The latter worried Theresa the most, and she was determined to prevent Amelia from making a rash decision. She owed it to Robert, both as a friend and a firefighter. He'd sacrificed his life for their community, and she'd vowed to see his widow through the worst of her grief. *I'll look after her, Robert. I promise.*

The truck drew to a stop, and she looked at Mason, who sat behind the wheel. His expression was stark, and his cheeks pale. He, too, felt the weight of Robert's death, having lost a friend and mentor. His loss differed from hers and Amelia's. Edged by guilt, it cut deep into his soul, tainting his every waking moment with useless questions and regrets.

Theresa felt for him. He was too young to know such sorrow, especially after losing both parents in a tragic fire. *I'll look after him, Robert. I'll look after all of them. I swear it.*

But no amount of promises would mean anything if she couldn't back it with action. And that was what she needed to do at that moment. Talk to the hospital leaders and ensure their people's survival.

"Give me a few moments, Mason. Let me talk to these people first," she said.

"Go ahead. I'll wait," he said with a quick nod.

Sucking in a deep breath, Theresa climbed out of the vehicle. She smoothed her hands over her jacket and walked toward the group waiting on the steps that led to the hospital's entrance.

Her back ached. She hadn't had a painkiller in days, and digging through the rubble of their former home hadn't helped matters. But she held her head high and walked with pride. While they might be refugees, forced to flee their home, they weren't beggars. They had much to offer to any community. Both supplies and skills. *I must make them see our worth.*

Striding toward the greeting party waiting to greet them, Theresa paused a few feet away and offered a firm smile. "Good day. I'm Theresa, the leader of our group. It's nice to finally meet you all."

A short, stocky woman wearing a navy blue blazer stepped forward. A pair of reading glasses perched on the tip of her nose, and her tight braids were swept back into a knot. The woman reached out her hand and said, "I am most pleased to meet you, Theresa. I'm Sophia, the director of this hospital. We spoke on the radio?"

"Indeed we did. Briefly," Theresa acknowledged as they shook hands.

"Well, I'm happy to welcome you and your people to our humble home," Sophia said.

"Thank you," Theresa said.

"I hope you don't mind, but anyone who's been outside these walls has to undergo a mandatory inspection before they can be allowed back inside the hospital," Sophia said.

"Of course. I expected nothing less," Theresa said.

"This is Madeleine. She's the head matron, and the hospital is her playground. The medical wards, at least. She'll oversee the inspections," Sophia said, introducing a stout woman in her late forties. "If anyone in your party needs medical care, she can take care of that too."

"We have an amputee and a few people suffering from minor burns, scrapes, bruises, and smoke inhalation. Nothing too serious, thankfully."

"I'll see they get treated immediately," Madeleine said with a firm nod. Dressed in a starched white uniform with not a hair out of place, she looked exactly like she would've before the apocalypse.

That told Theresa something about the way things were run in the hospital. They were likely sticklers for the rules and etiquette, clinging to the old ways. While she didn't think that was necessarily bad, she did wonder how long it would last.

"We've set up a ward for you to share, and there are enough beds and blankets for everyone," Sophia said. "It's only temporary, though. We'll work out a more permanent solution soon."

221

"I'm sure it will be fine," Theresa reassured her.

"There are bathrooms down the hall, a common room, a cafeteria, and the gardens. Please, make yourselves at home," Sophia said.

Theresa nodded. "Thank you. I'm sure we'll be very comfortable."

"It's not your old home, but we'll do our best to welcome you. That's a promise," Sophia said with a kind smile. "Lindsey, our head cook, is preparing a feast in your honor as we speak."

"You shouldn't have," Theresa said, taken aback.

"It's nothing over the top," Sophia said with a wave of the hand. "Just a little get-together. The perfect opportunity for our two communities to meet and mingle."

"That's very thoughtful of you," Theresa said.

"You need not worry about your safety either," Lt. Kingsley said, stepping forward. "My team and I work hard to ensure everyone here is safe and secure."

"What about our weapons?" Theresa asked, a tight knot of anxiety forming in her stomach.

"Only the guards are allowed to carry guns," Lt. Kingsley said. "As such, you will have to hand over any firearms for safekeeping."

"I'm not sure we can do that," Theresa said, shaking her head. "We lost people because the infection got in and our weapons were locked up. If we'd been armed, we could've stopped it from going that far."

"I understand that, but it's our policy. You can carry a hand weapon for self-defense, but no firearms."

"I see," Theresa said.

"As long as you realize that using such a weapon against another community member means immediate expulsion,"

Sophia added.

"We can keep our knives and fire axes, then?" Theresa asked. "Purely for self-defense?"

"Yes. One weapon per person, adults only," Kingsley confirmed.

"We would also like to integrate some of your people into our ranks which means they'd be allowed to bear arms," Sophia said.

"Alright," Theresa said, realizing there wasn't much choice. She had no room for negotiation, and they had nowhere else to go. "I accept."

"Thank you for understanding," Sophia said. "Lt. Kingsley will gather the firearms and store them in our weapon's locker. Should you wish to leave, they will be returned."

"What if we want to go on a supply run?" Theresa asked. "Or leave the hospital grounds for any other reason?"

"You can clear it with the lieutenant, and he'll ensure you are properly armed," Sophia answered. "As long as you surrender them upon your return, it won't be a problem."

"Alright," Theresa said, relieved to know they'd still have a modicum of freedom.

"Stella here will show you to your quarters. She's in charge of housekeeping," Sophia added.

A woman with faded red hair and grey eyes stepped forward. Slender and sinewy, she looked as tough as nails. "I ensured everything was clean and sanitized, including the bedding and towels. I also provided some basic toiletries, but if you need anything else, please ask."

"I think we'll be okay for now," Theresa said. "Each person packed a bag with the necessities before we left."

"Excellent," Sophia said, handing Theresa a flip file filled with papers. "You'll find the house rules, the dining room schedule, the laundry and cleaning schedule, the shower and bath roster, and the electricity timetable inside. Everything is strictly monitored and rationed. Our resources are limited, and we can't afford to waste anything."

"Understood," Theresa said, taking the file and casting an eye over the neat handwriting. She could appreciate proper paperwork. It appealed to the control freak inside her brain.

"We've also cleared space for your vehicles in the lot, and Coco will show you where to park," Sophia said. "If you have mechanical problems, she's the one to talk to."

Theresa nodded at Coco. "You're a mechanic?"

"Yup," Coco said, her lips popping on the p. A flash of silver exposed a tongue ring, and both arms were covered in tattoos. Sleeves, Theresa believed they were called. They matched her spiky black hair, oil-stained jeans, and combat boots.

"Good. We could use one," Theresa said, unfazed by the woman's tough looks.

Coco grinned. "I'm sure you do. Especially one as good as me." With those words, she waved at Mason. "Follow me, handsome."

She sauntered away with a swing to her hips, and Theresa smothered a grin. *I think I'm going to like Coco.*

Mason stuck his head out the window and asked, "What do I do, Theresa?"

"Do what the lady says," Theresa said, still smiling.

Mason ducked back inside with a shrug and drove after Coco. The convoy followed him, each heading toward their allotted parking spot.

"I think that's everything," Sophia said. "Unless you have any more questions?"

224

"What about our supplies? Where can we store them?" Theresa asked.

"Supplies? You brought supplies?" Sophia asked with a hint of surprise.

"Yes. We managed to salvage quite a bit from the wreckage," Theresa said, not mentioning the extra stuff they'd hidden away in a safe house.

It had been Frank's idea to have a secret stash of food, water, medicine, and other essential supplies stored in a secure location. It would act as a bug-out location should they need it and provide them with a temporary haven in case of an emergency.

Most of their guns and ammunition had been stored there, along with what remained of their fireman's gear, fire axes, a few drums of fuel, a couple of vehicles, and one fire truck. There were also a few crates of food, bottled water, clothing, bedding, medicine, toiletries, and camping gear.

The whole lot was stored inside an old warehouse, and the windows and doors were reinforced and locked tight. It was situated on the edge of town in a derelict district that offered little in the way of scavenging. Hopefully, it would remain undetected.

While Theresa wanted to get along with their new community, she'd agreed to the plan. It was never a good idea to have all one's eggs in the same basket, and it paid to be prepared. She'd made certain they brought enough to the hospital to show their worth, however, and their willingness to contribute. While it hurt to give it all up, it was for a good cause.

"Well, I wasn't expecting you to bring anything, but I welcome the assistance," Sophia said with a nod. "I'll send a couple of people to help you offload and take the stuff to storage. You are welcome to keep anything you might need, though."

"I think we're alright for now, but if we need anything, we'll ask," Theresa said.

"Excellent. I hope that covers everything. If you'll excuse me, I'm needed elsewhere," Sophia said, clearly in a hurry.

"Of course. I wouldn't want to keep you," Theresa said.

"It was nice meeting you," Sophia said before she rushed away.

Theresa was left feeling deflated. While she hadn't expected a hero's welcome, she'd hoped for a warmer reception. That was what the supplies were for, after all. But Sophia didn't seem impressed. *She didn't even bother to take a look at what we brought. They must have it pretty easy over here.*

At that moment, Theresa felt like she and her people were the poor relations of the family. Tolerated but not truly wanted. There wasn't much she could do about it, however. They had nowhere else to go and no one to turn to. *We'll just have to make the best of it. There's no other way.*

As the rest of the convoy drove through the gates, Theresa scraped together her flagging dignity and helped everyone find their place.

A woman called Lindsay arrived with a couple of helpers to unload the supplies and take them to storage. At least she was more appreciative, her eyebrows raising when she counted all the crates. "Wow, when Sophia said you needed help, I figured you had a few boxes at most. I'd better get the rest of the crew here to help."

That made Theresa feel better, and she hoped the news would filter through to Sophia. *If not, I'll make sure it does.*

The same could not be said of their weapons cache. They'd

lost a lot in the fire, and most of that was stashed away in the warehouse. They had just enough left for it not to look suspicious, and Lt. Kingsley and his team collected it without comment.

Coco inspected the vehicles, flagging a number for future repairs, while everyone underwent a physical exam in the trauma center. Those that needed medical treatment were taken to a separate ward, while the rest were shown to their quarters.

The entire affair was very business-like and efficient. It also felt cold and unsympathetic. The only bright spot in the process was the paramedic Zoey, who welcomed everyone with a cheery smile. She dragged her fellow medic Banks around by the arm, a forced grin plastered on his face, while she babbled nonstop.

It would've been funny if Theresa didn't feel so depressed. It was hard to ignore all the sad faces around her. Thankfully, no one complained out loud. There was no point, after all.

A few people hung back, reluctant to give up their freedom, but when the gates clanged shut, an air of finality fell over the gathering. One by one, everyone turned away with looks of muted despair, and Theresa knew she had her work cut out for her.

She marched into the hospital, squaring her shoulders, trying to set an example for the rest. *We'll make it work. We have to.*

End of excerpt. Get your copy today!
  Hold the Line - Heroes of the Apocalypse Book 4
  https://www.amazon.com/dp/B0B6J2553H

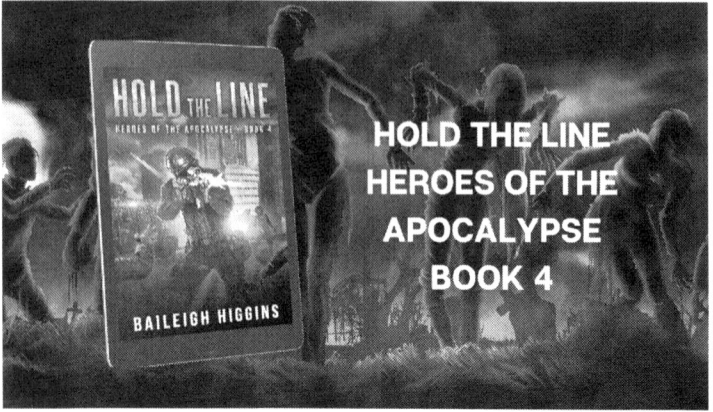

HOLD THE LINE
HEROES OF THE
APOCALYPSE
BOOK 4

Your FREE EBook is waiting!

If you'd like to learn more about my books, upcoming projects, new releases, cover reveals, and promotions, simply join my mailing list. Plus, you'll get an exclusive ebook absolutely FREE just for subscribing!

Yes, please. Sign me up!
https://www.subscribepage.com/i0d7r8

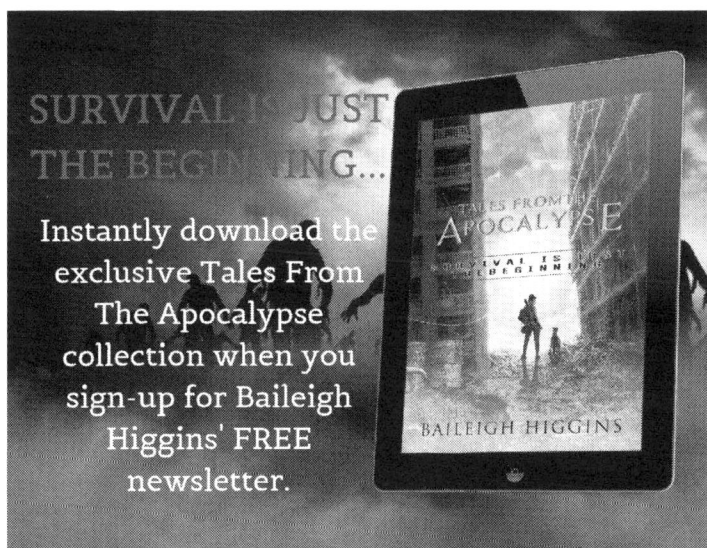

SURVIVAL IS JUST THE BEGINNING...

Instantly download the exclusive Tales From The Apocalypse collection when you sign-up for Baileigh Higgins' FREE newsletter.

BAILEIGH HIGGINS

About the Author

AUTHOR OF THE APOCALYPSE

South African writer and coffee addict, Baileigh Higgins, lives in the Free State with hubby and best friend Brendan and loves nothing more than lazing on the couch with pizza and a bad horror movie. Her unhealthy obsession with the end of the world has led to numerous books on the subject and a secret bunker only she knows the location of.

Visit her website at www.baileighhiggins.com for more information on her upcoming projects, new releases, and giveaways. Sign up for her Newsletter and get your Free Ebook, Tales from the Apocalypse, today.

SURVIVAL IS JUST THE BEGINNING

WEBSITE: https://www.baileighhiggins.com

Printed in Great Britain
by Amazon